DAMAGED SERIES

RUSSIAN DOG

Cynthia Seidel

Fulton Books
Meadville, PA

Published by Fulton Books 2024

ISBN 979-8-88982-754-2 (paperback)
ISBN 979-8-88982-755-9 (digital)

Printed in the United States of America

To my beautiful husband, Kro, who believed
this book into reality. I love you most.

Annika Volkov

At twenty-seven years old, I should be married with 2.5 kids by now. Instead, I was locked up in this mansion like some princess in a fairy tale. My life was a living hell and did not come close to resembling a happily ever after.

My life was torn apart at the age of six. My father threw my mother over a three-story balcony to her death as I watched in horror. My mother was trying to protect me from my father's wrath as she always did. In the end, it was futile. I wet the bed again, and one of the housekeepers informed my father. He always told my mother it was because I was spoiled and lazy. The truth was probably more of his fault than he wanted to admit. He would punish me as he always did, with his fists. My mother stepped in to protect me, and it cost her life. My mother suffered mental and physical abuse at the hands of my father for most of her life. In a horrific way, she was now freer than she had ever been.

Women in the Mafia were nothing more than pawns on a chessboard. At least in the Russian Mafia, that's the way it was. Women had no voice, no dreams, and no quality of life of their own. We were owned by our fathers until we were traded or bargained for contracts, alliances, money, and even for debt.

Over the years, I had done my best to be invisible. I kept my head down and my mouth shut. I only came out of my room to attend college classes.

I was groomed to be an obedient daughter at a young age. To do as I was told without any question. When I say groomed, I do mean he beat the hell out of me until I submitted. He made sure I was so scared of him that I would never tell a soul what he had done to my poor mother.

I mean nothing to my father. To him, I was his ignorant failure. For one, he wanted a son, and he got me. Second, I had learning issues caused by dyslexia. I needed tutors my entire life to help me learn to deal with my learning disability. And he reminded me every chance he got how stupid I was.

"You're stupid and ugly, just like your whore mother" was what he always said. I came to believe over the years that there must be some truth to his words. I was not sure what smart or beautiful looked like.

At five eight, I was taller than most women. I had long thick blond hair that went to my waist. It was hard to manage most of the time. My eyes were a weird color of blue. They were almost gray. They were so light. I was extremely thin for my height, around a hundred pounds. My father always said, "You can't be stupid, ugly and, fat." So he managed my food intake. I usually got a salad for dinner, and that was all, if I got that. My bodyguards reported back to my father if I tried to get anything outside the house.

That's not where the abuse stopped. There was more, much more. He started sexually abusing me when I was ten, taking my innocence and leaving me with humiliation that would last a lifetime.

I tried to fight back a couple of times over the years, and it left me more broken in the end. When I was thirteen, he assaulted me, and I got sick and threw up all over him. After beating the hell out of me where I kneeled, he grabbed a fistful of my hair and dragged me to the basement. It was a place where he tortured his prisoners, a place I knew all too well. He chained my hands above my head. My toes barely touched the ground. And then he cut my clothes off. I was there for four days, cold, hungry, and battered. He took a horse-whip to me all four of those days, leaving me scarred physically and mentally. I never fought him again after that day. I was truly broken, a shell of the person I should have been.

My saving grace was my used-to-be nanny, Vera. She was now our housekeeper and my only friend. She talked my father into allowing me to attend college. She explained to him that it could help me with my dyslexia. He was happy to get me out of his hair until he needed me to take his anger out on. Part of me thought that allowing me to attend classes was his way of dealing with any guilt he might have for the things he did to me.

When I was nineteen, I started classes toward a medical degree. I struggled, but I didn't feel stupid. I just felt like I had to learn another way. In two months, I would be finished with medical school and be Dr. Annika Volkov. And the funny thing was, my father had no clue. He assumed I just took classes and volunteered at the hospital to get out of the house. I applied for my residency at a couple hospitals and prayed I would get accepted. I was not sure what was after that because my father would never let me work. I must find a way out.

Angelino Rossi

Five years earlier

I had never been a man to settle for one woman for long. Yes, I dated a few times, but I didn't get attached. When I got bored, I moved on. One such woman was Bianca Monroe, my typical type of woman. She had long dark hair, a curvy body, and dark brown eyes. She was beautiful. But also, with the woman I dated came the money-hungry, self-absorbed, and entitled brats that they were. Something I never really cared for in a woman.

I came to realize Bianca was hooked on cocaine and had been for years. I ended the relationship, and we both went our separate ways. Well, until she showed up on the doorstep of my penthouse strung out and holding an infant. I was thirty at the time.

"Here. She is yours," she said, shoving the baby into my arms.

I looked at her, shocked for a few seconds, and said, "What are you doing?"

"She is sick and won't stop crying. I don't have the patience to handle her. I figured you would want her instead of me giving her to some strangers."

I knew what she meant by sick. My daughter was addicted.

"Of course, I want her if she's mine. You don't want her?"

"No, she is all yours. I have no place for a child in my life. I have my own dreams to live."

"What is her name?"

"She does not have one. I gave birth to her yesterday, and I did not name her because I'm not keeping her."

At this moment, I knew several reasons I did not get attached to a woman like her.

"Then be on your way and never return," I told her, closing the door in her face. What happened to good and loving women? Ones that loved their children and would move heaven and earth for their families?

"Hey there, little girl. Looks like I'm your daddy. It's good to meet you," I said, kissing her red screaming face. I called our family doctor and explained what was going on and that I needed him to meet me at the house in the clinic. The clinic was an emergency room in the basement of our mansion.

I arrived at the clinic and handed the screaming infant to the doc. He examined her and drew some blood for a DNA test and to find out what was going on with her. He handed her back to me while he was testing her blood. I patted her on the back as I walked around the room with her, trying to soothe her.

"Shhh, little girl, it's going to be okay. You are with your daddy now."

"She does still have cocaine in her system. She is also premature. I'm not sure how she got her out of the hospital like this. She needs intensive care for several weeks. I am calling Chicago Memorial to have a room set up for her with round-the-clock care. I'll make sure you can stay with her."

"Thank you, Doc. We will head there now."

We got to the hospital, and the hospital staff took over her care. She was hooked up to so many wires for such a little thing. The doctor gave my daughter some meds and got her to settle down. I got to feed her for the first time. I spoke to her sweetly and kissed her little head. They placed her back in isolation.

"Get some rest, little one."

I sat down in the chair next to her and let everything sink in. The doc would call me and let me know the results of the DNA test. But I already knew she was mine. Bianca knew better than to ever cross me. She knew who I was and who my family was.

"Now you need a name," I said more to myself than to my daughter. Grazia Marie Rossi. Grazia meant "grace" in Italian, and it was fitting.

My brothers, Antonio and Giovani, came by several times to relieve me so I could shower and eat. My brothers had been my whole world since I could remember. Antonio was the oldest, and Giovani was the baby. Our parents put us all through hell. Neither one was suitable to be parents. They were both cruel and suited each other. If one wasn't tormenting us, then the other was. Our father had us killing rivals at a young age. I was eight when I was first made to pull the trigger and take a man's life. My mother stood there and laughed with cruelty. We had been locked in that basement to torture. My father called it tough love. He was making us men, was what he always said. My mother didn't even give us an excuse for the sadistic things she did. She burned us with cigarettes and struck us with a metal rod. A couple of things among many. We always said we would not let them break us. When we grew up, we would be better men for those who needed us. That was my plan with Grazia. My parents wouldn't taint her like they did my brothers and me.

Grazia was in the hospital for several weeks. The doctor said she might have some health issues and learning disabilities. We would get through it all. I was just happy when I finally got to take her home.

Angelino Rossi

"This has been the hardest six months of my life," I said to my little brother, Giovanni. "I never wanted any of this. I never wanted to be the head of the Italian Mafia. Antonio was always so good at it. He was made to lead. I was meant to be the second-in-command, not a don. How could things have gotten so fucked up?"

Our oldest brother, Antonio, was killed in a bombing six months ago by Petrov Volkov, a Russian don who had been pushing for our territory for years. Volkov tried to pin the killing on the Chicago MC and the Greeks from Philadelphia by planting evidence pointing that way. We knew different.

"I know how you feel, brother. This a nightmare I can never wake up from."

"I don't have the easygoing, laid-back attitude Antonio had. I don't want to have to take a wife for a male heir. Antonio looked forward to settling down. This was his burden to bear, not mine," I said in an angry tone.

"I can't see you with one woman for the rest of your life. You will be like a caged animal," Giovanni said, laughing.

"Thank God I am only thirty-five. I will put it off as long as possible."

"You can always take a mistress or two. Dad always did."

"I am not my father. I may never love my wife, but I would never disrespect her like that. Mother was a bitch, but I know the affairs still hurt her. I will never be able to do that to a woman.

"Enough talk of women. Let's get down to business," I said.

Giovanni nodded in agreement and said, "We have let the dust settle for six months, allowing our enemies to think we don't know who murdered our brother and will not attempt retribution. Now is the time to watch our enemy fall. We need to get our cousins here and go over our plan to end Volkov. I don't want to just kill him. I want to destroy him and his legacy. I want to shut him down and take everything that belongs to him."

"We need to be smart about this. I think we need to bring the best cyber geek we know and have a head of cybernetics. Luca has mad skills on a computer. That man is in his own little world of data," I said, laughing.

Luca Rossi was one of five of our cousins. At six three and 250 lbs. of muscle, Luca did not look like a computer nerd. Like all of us, he was covered in tattoos and had black hair and eyes.

We decided after our father was killed a year and a half ago to bring our cousins into the fold.

"I want this to be handled like a military mission. We have a cyber tech. Now we need a head of security. I want all new high-tech security systems installed on all our properties. I want every person to have GPS tracking chips inserted on their bodies so we can locate our men if they are taken. We could have saved Antonio if he had one. We need to start recruiting more men and start a training program. I want everyone to have martial arts or combat skills. We need someone over finances, buying properties, investing, building more legit businesses. We place our cousins over divisions, and then they can divide responsibilities to people they trust. I want this to run like a corporation, a well-oiled machine," I said.

"Maybe some casinos and a few restaurants along with the strip clubs we already have. But we have done well over the last year and a half to put off profit in the billions. I say we end the skin trade now that we are well ahead," Giovani explained.

Our father started the skin trade decades ago. It was something my brothers and I didn't believe in. Women selling themselves to live and us profiting off them was not something I could live with. Our plan was to relocate the women to anywhere they wanted to go and set them up in homes they would own and pay for them to get on their feet, either through college or businesses they may want to open.

"I agree. Let's pull the trigger on this part of our plan and shut the skin trade down. I want to keep the contacts our father had with the women, but I would like to purchase bigger shipments of weapons and tactical gear instead. We are going to need them."

Giovanna sat back in his chair and took a sip of his whiskey. "What do you think of not just bringing our cousins in to help but making them partners and advisers? I think if they had some skin in the game and not just help us out, the Rossis will be the only ruling family in Chicago. That way, we all rule and have heirs, and they take over the same as us, bringing our entire plan together like we have always talked about."

"I like it, but keep the power equal. Majority gets the vote. Not all the power goes to one man or the spoils. We will be harder to take down," I said.

"Our vision is becoming a reality. What else is on the plan?" asked Giovanni.

"To end the extortion of our people. We three agreed that we don't want to be rich by stepping on the throats of our own people. We should protect our people without being paid for it. I think that will bring more loyalty and respect than fear ever will. The ones who should fear us are our enemies, not our own people."

"Doing things differently than other Mafia families will make us appear weak. We will have the loyalty of our men and our community. That alone our enemies should fear," said Giovanni.

"I will set up the meeting with our cousins for tomorrow," I said.

"Uncle Gio! Uncle Gio!" Grazia screamed as she came running in the room. Giovanni leaned over his chair and scooped her into his lap.

"Well, don't you look pretty today," Gio gushed. "What have you been doing all day?"

"Having a tea party with Mia." Mia was Grazia's nanny and had been since I brought Grazia home. "Mia and I both dressed up as princesses."

Mia laughed from the doorway. "Give your dad and uncle a hug good night and let's get you ready for bed."

Grazia pouted and looked at her father and asked, "Can't I stay up five more minutes?"

"Mia said it's bedtime, so give me a hug good night and do as you're told, young lady. I will be up to tuck you in shortly."

Grazia did as she was told and headed upstairs with Mia.

"She sure is growing up fast," Giovanni said.

I ran my hand down my face and said with an eye roll, "Tell me about it."

"Well, all this talk of change and prosperity has worn me out. I'm heading to my room. Good night, brother," Giovanni said as he headed to his apartment in the east wing of the mansion.

The mansion was hundreds of years old and was a former castle of some nobleman. The Rossi family bought it over a hundred years ago. It was three stories high and had three wings on each floor—the east wing, the west wing, and the north wing. Each wing had several apartments in each, and all were huge. The mansion contained an indoor atrium, library, gym, theater, an operating clinic, and a dungeon. The outside had a huge pool, beach, a shooting range, and a training facility. The perimeter was surrounded by concrete walls, except for the back of the mansion, where the beach of Lake Michigan was. We secured it with more guards.

As Giovanni walked to his wing of the house, he thought to himself, *By looking at this place, you would think me and my brother would have loved growing up here.*

The mansion was amazing, but if the walls could talk, they would tell of a story of abuse and pain. It would tell of times when my brothers and I were locked in the dungeon for days, the same place my father brought his prisoners. Our backs could still feel the sting of the whip and the burn of hot metal, all in the name of making boys into strong and powerful men.

My parents did not believe in love. They believed in money and power and respect. My father did not care how he obtained it. Most of it was on the back of his people through fear and pain. And that was what got him killed over a year ago.

Our father hated women. Well, except for sex, and in that, he was even abusive. He was never faithful to my mother, but with his twisted ways, I was sure she was happy he went elsewhere for it. He tortured his women brutally. He taught us to manage a woman in the same way. My brothers and I could never stomach the abuse of the innocent. It never sat right with any of us.

Angelino

I headed up to tuck my daughter in for the night. It was hard to believe how much you could love one little person. She had been my entire world since the day she was laid in my arms. These had been the best five years of my life, watching her grow. She might be a tiny little thing, but she was fierce. I thought of how a parent could ever be abusive to something so innocent and pure.

I headed to the west wing of the mansion, where my apartment was located, and sat in a chair on the balcony and replayed the conversation my brother and I had. It reminded me of how my parents were and how different my brothers and I were from them. When my father died, I was happy to see him lowered to the ground. He was killed by the Russians, and it was ironic because he acted just like them. He had no shame, no self-respect, and no honor. He lived by no code. He murdered women and children and stood on the backs of his people to gain power. My mother was no better than my father and was still alive and as hateful as ever.

When Grazia came into my life, I spent my first four years with her in my penthouse to keep her away from my parents. Then my father died a year ago, and my brothers and I moved back in the mansion, but not before sitting our mother down and giving her all the new rules. She no longer had any power. We allowed her to run the household, but nothing else. She was threatened. If she ever laid a finger on my daughter, she would pay with her life.

My daughter would always have a better life and a choice in how it was lived. This life should not be for everyone if they did not choose it. My brothers and I decided when our father died how we wanted to run the family, and even though Antonio was gone, we would still move forward with our plans to rule over this city in a way no generation before us ever had. It was time for a new era of Mafia leaders, ones who set fear in the hearts of their enemy and loyalty from their own people.

After we take down Volkov, we would end his reign and shut down all the Russian scum. The rest would have no choice but to flee the city or be killed. There was no room for two families to rule here. Volkov had been murdering our people and slowly taking over the city. My father just let it happen. But me, I won't let sleeping dogs lie. I was the reaper. I would bring revenge and death to all who stand in my way. To my family, I was love, protection, and loyalty. To my enemies, I was fear, death, and destruction.

My brothers and I were all huge men. We did inherit that from our father, along with a nasty temper. I was six four and 275 lbs. of muscle. With all my tattoos, I was a menacing sight to my enemies. To women, I was the bad boy in their wet dreams. My dark hair and eyes alone could get me into any woman's panties. God knows I've had several of them. None of them were allowed at my house. We met at a hotel or at my penthouse in the city. The woman I fucked or dated were not worthy of meeting my sweet Garza. They either wanted to be my queen for status and money or my huge cock. Like Jessica. She was stunning. She was about five five and about 120 lbs., with dark brown hair and brown eyes. She had huge tits, probably a D. And she was the most self-absorbed woman I had ever met. But she was fuckable, and that was it. She tried to act classy with her stilettos and sexy dresses, but class wasn't something you could turn on when you wanted. It was instilled in you when you were young. To me, she acted like a high-dollar call girl. But she was beautiful and would do when the need arose. And believe me, it arose often.

Annika

As I studied for the last of my exams, I started to feel sad. I should be so excited that I finished all my clinicals and exams by the end of the week. I would be graduating with a 4.0 and have my medical degree. But knowing my father, he would never allow me to get my residency to become a surgeon. I was very proud I completed medical school and would become a doctor. But would I ever get the chance to use it? I had been accepted into Chicago Memorial's residency program to become a surgeon. That would start in six months. I just didn't know how I was going to convince him to allow it. My father had no idea what I had been going to college for. Truth be known, he had not cared. He thought I volunteered at the hospital a few days a week to get out of the house. But the residency would take on all hours of the day and night, and I couldn't hide that. If I ran, he would find me. I just prayed that one day, I would get out of this hell and be loved by someone.

The way things have been going the last couple of weeks with my father, I might not live long enough to see any of my dreams come true. I was almost thirty and had never had a life. Was this life worth living if I couldn't get out? I knew it was not, and I couldn't do it forever. My father had been angrier the last couple of weeks, more than usual. The rape was accompanied by pure violence and abuse. He was angry and was taking it out on me. I had several broken bones and stitches over the last couple of weeks.

Last night, I came out with ten more stiches on my head, and he broke my left hand and three ribs on my left side. Good thing for my father, we had our own doctor. The doctor set my wrist and stitched me up again. When I passed my father in the foyer while heading to class, he just looked at my wrist and rolled his eyes, like he couldn't believe I was that pathetic and weak that my hand broke. I just put my head down and walked as quickly as I could to the car.

Angelino

Over the last month, we put our plan together to take down Volkov and started acting. Giovanni and I spoke to our six cousins and brought them into our fold. Our fathers were brothers and were one and the same—cruel, ruthless, uncaring men. We had that in common among wanting to see Volkov fall. Each one of us had our own set of skills, attitudes, and connections, but together, we had what it took to run an empire. I trusted each one of these men with my life. With us bringing them in, we were setting ourselves up for success. It was much harder to take over an empire that was not run by one man but seven, but we ruled as one. We would own this entire city when we were done. What else would you need in a war?

Luca was our intel tech. He was thirty and smart. He could find anything out on any person. He had mad skills in computer technology. He had an IQ of 190 and was the smartest man I knew. He once broke into the government's encrypted files. They tried to come after him for it, but all the evidence they had against him disappeared. He broke into FBI security and wiped everything when he saw them snooping. That went over like a ton of bricks. To Luca, it was a big game of who was smarter, and of course, he was.

Dante was the oldest of our cousins. He was the same age as me. He is six three also. Dante was a big guy, just not as broad as Luca. He had a scar on the right side of his face, starting at his hairline and going down to his chin. It was a nice gift his father gave him when he was eleven for not wanting to cut a man's tongue out. His father turned him into who he was today, and that's where his special skills came in. He was a dealer of pain. His own tortured soul made him suited for this job.

The youngest of the brothers was Rocco, and he was a force to be reckoned with. At six foot six and three hundred pounds of tattooed muscle, he looked like a wall of muscle coming at you. He was twenty-eight years old and had his own security business already. He wanted a way out of his father's life. He was a natural protector and the one who stopped the abuse of their father. He had been huge even as a child. At the age of thirteen, he was bigger than his father. At the age of fifteen, Rocco had enough. He was knocking his brother Luca around, who was seventeen at the time. His father hated Luca because he was into computers, and he was always calling him a pussy. Rocco stepped in and grabbed his father by the throat. He picked him up and slammed him to the ground. His father was in shock. He never laid a hand on any of the boys again. His father might have been the second-in-command, but he was a bitch. He only hurt those who could not protect themselves. Rocco was a protector of his family, a big teddy bear with the women, and a force to his enemies.

Then there were the twins, Matteo and Santos, both thirty-two years old and total opposites.

Matteo, or "pretty boy," as his brothers like to call him, was also intelligent. He was very good at business. He was six three and 240 lbs. of lean muscle. He was extremely fast and agile. He loved martial arts and was proficient in two different types. If he hit you, you would never see it coming. He never had a hair out of place. It was neat and combed back, and he always had on a tailored suit. With his full lips and long lashes, the women would never leave him alone. He spent more time primping than most women did. He was a pretty boy. He already had a couple of businesses of his own and was doing well for himself. He was brought in, along with his twin, to handle their businesses, to help expand and grow.

Santos was the tortured soul. He used to be the comedian of the family until he was eleven, and something changed. He was full of rage and didn't speak much. He was also six three. He was more muscle than Matteo. He weight lifted and was 260 lbs. He was also into mixed martial arts. Instead of suits, he loved his T-shirts and jeans. He had long curly and shaggy hair, and he had blue eyes instead of brown. Santos was rough around the edges. He was very intelligent like his brother and had a head for business, but he preferred a hands-on approach. He owned a popular boxing and martial arts gym and was a member of Chicago's MC. He loved riding his Harley and the freedom it brought to his life. He would help with the business and training parts of the business.

Over the last several weeks, Giovanni and I set up the heads of our table with all our cousins. We met several times over the weeks and started implementing our plan to take down Volkov's entire operation and continue growing our legitimate business. Matteo and Santos were working on investing the money we had in stocks and properties, buying up land to build casinos and luxury condos and a couple of high-end strip clubs to add to the couple we already had.

We chose managers of the strip clubs we already had going. It would keep us out of the day-to-day operations and into more important things.

Jasper was now the manager of Vixen. He used to be a manager in one of our restaurants that the Russians burned down. He understood the business part of it well and would be an asset.

We chose Laya to manage the Honey Hole. She worked closely with Santos to bring an end to the skin trade. Laya was one of the women in our father's whorehouses. After speaking to several of the women we set free, we decided to ask Laya about a position in one of the clubs. All the women said she went out of her way to protect all of them. Laya took the manager position and an apartment that was provided with the new position. She explained that it was only temporary until she could get her college education. We all agreed, and we were also paying for her degree. She worked with us to get all the women home or a place to live until they got on their feet. Some came from across the world, and we would help them get back there.

Laya had no family of her own. She was an orphan from Hawaii. Laya and another girl were abducted heading back to the orphanage after school. She was only fourteen when she was abducted. She was auctioned off to a man from New York that was a wealthy banker. He bought her for her virginity and to have as a toy to play with. When she turned sixteen, he tired of her, and she was sold to a whorehouse.

She remained there until the Rossis set her free recently. She was used at the whorehouse for five years. Now she had a shot at a real life. And she was going to make good use of it and help others.

Giovanni and I also worked on building trust in our community. We walked throughout our community to meet each shop owner and to speak with them personally. Our father did a lot of damage to the community by taking protective money from them. These people were just trying to make a living. Because our father extorted money, there was no trust from the community. We explained to each shop owner that they were under our protection, but they would never have to pay protection money again, and anyone who needed help could come to us for anything. By doing this and getting the trust of our people, we would always have their loyalty.

One of the pizza places was having issues with the old electrical in the building, so Giovanni and I contacted our contractors and had them start renovating the pizza shop up to their expectation. We gave the family enough money to survive on while the shop was being worked on. How good it felt to be able to help others, I thought to myself, instead of watching my father crush and steal people's hopes. Yes, indeed this was going to be the start of something no one could comprehend.

We worked with Luca and Rocco on getting security set up. And not just any security. We were installing a control room at the mansion that would monitor everything 24-7. It could also be monitored from anywhere else from any person on the team. All access to the houses was through a high security system that used handprints with a code to enter. They added more cameras and motion detectors around the wall and front gate. All vehicles were now bulletproof. Luca also had an operating system as high-tech as they came. You could find out almost anything from anywhere. Being a hacker had its advantages.

Each person on our team and family, including ourselves, were injected with micro GPS trackers. They inserted them in different locations on each person. Luca could find anyone anywhere. It did have its limitations through heavy metal buildings. In this business, you could never be too careful. The family had several men at our disposal. What we wanted was an army, one that could take and hold the territory from the Russians. We started recruiting people. Our team members started bringing in people we trusted as part of the security. They would be placed all over the city in plain sight to watch and protect over our people. The rest of the people worked with us on shutting down Volkov's operations. He would no longer be able to take what was already ours. We were ready when they tried to take anything that was in our territory.

Last week, there was an attempt to burn down the Honey Hole, one of our strip clubs. But the facial software we were using picked up a couple of their goons in our territory, and it put our team on alert. We stopped them before anything could even happen.

And now we had two of their goons in the holding area, which was our basement in the mansion. We left them down there in the basement for several days without food and water. Dante was sent down to interrogate both goons.

"What did you learn from the guards, Dante?" I asked.

"That the two goons we captured are low-level guys. They didn't have a whole lot to say, except for Volkov having a daughter that he is obsessed with, and she's not allowed out of the house except for classes, and then she has to return."

"How old is the daughter?"

"She is twenty-seven years old. And by the looks of it, he has no plans to marry her off. He plans to keep her. My assumption is that he loves his daughter very much and does not want her married off to some asshole. One of the goons used to be her bodyguard. He said the girl is very sheltered and only allowed to take some college classes and volunteer at a local hospital. Then she has to come directly home and back to her room. The guard said he is so protective of his daughter. One of the old guards looked at his daughter in the wrong way, and he killed him. The guard said he was surprised that Volkov allowed his daughter to take classes. But Volkov always said his daughter was an idiot, so he was trying to educate her," Dante said.

"Very interesting. I might be able to use this to our advantage," I said.

We also put a plan together last week to have several teams ready to hit Russian businesses and warehouses at the same time. If we did it all once, they would not be prepared for our attack. Volkov dealt a lot in the skin trade at his whorehouses and at his auctions. We couldn't put him out of business completely until he was dead, but right now, I wanted him to suffer. I wanted him to lose millions. I wanted him to get sloppy and arrogant. I wanted him to come crawling to me for an alliance. A fake alliance, but he did not need to know that.

A few days later, we decided when Volkov had lost so much to us and he wanted an alliance and peace because he was losing so badly and think it was all the Greeks or MC, I was going to take his daughter. I would marry her, not for love because she was a Russian whore, and a stupid one, by the sound of it. But I didn't need her smart to ruin her. I was going to make her pay for her father's sins. I was sure she was a spoiled little princess who got everything she wanted. He'd watch how his sweet little daughter would be broken by my hand. And then I would kill him and the second-in-command and anyone else that stood in my way. I'd make her sign it all over to me. Everything that belonged to her father would be mine. And then I'd release her into the world with nothing. They would all be ruined when I was done with them. Volkov's bloodline would be no more.

We put our teams together. We had four teams, each with a leader to take down some of Volkov's properties. One was an abandoned school. They used to house the women at one end, and the other end was used as a whorehouse. The women that were housed here were used in the whorehouse and at their strip clubs. It was heavily guarded, and security cameras were everywhere. More to keep the girls in than for people coming out. Luca had it set up to knock the cameras out and then gain us entry. After Luca monitored the security systems for over a week, we counted six armed guards we needed to take out. There were twenty-eight women that needed to be rescued. We had a driver and a large box truck ready to put the women in and get them to safety. Then we would burn this property and the strip club, warehouse, and any other property we were working on that night to the ground. After we made sure it was clear of innocents.

The fourth location was a huge warehouse Volkov used to store large amounts of weapons and drugs they had shipped in and were waiting for distribution. The property had a twelve-foot fence with razor wire at the top of it. It had one large gate at the front with two armed security guards. Luca tapped into the security cameras and confirmed the storage areas for the weapons and drugs. Eighteen-wheelers were ready to move in and remove everything Volkov had stored. It would not shut him down, but it would hurt him momentarily and unsettle him. That way, they could knock him off his pedestal.

There was an area in the warehouse that the men kept going in and out of a few times a day. But there were no cameras in the room. We assumed they were holding someone in the room. They brought food in a couple of times a week. We were sure to find out who it was.

The fifth location or locations were three businesses Volkov laundered his money through. He was strong-arming one business to get them to launder his money. It was a high-end restaurant. The Shift was known throughout the city. Lily James started the restaurant five years prior and had grown it into what it was today, a five-star restaurant. Luca found out the Russians were threatening her family unless she laundered their money. She must be moved to a new location, and we needed to protect her family because her place would be leveled to the ground also. We needed to get the restaurant out of the Russian territory until we took the whole city over. We did not want the Russians to know that we were taking down their properties. We wanted them to think it was another family he pissed off.

The other two properties was a strip club and a bakery Volkov owned.

The plan was to be fully masked and in tactical gear for this mission. All trucks would be ready for pickup at all locations, and separate smaller teams would burn the strip clubs down and the bakery and restaurant they used. They would use headsets to communicate, and we'd go in all at the same time so Volkov would not be tipped off. Volkov wouldn't know what hit him, and he'd assume that the Albanians or Greek mob he had been trying to take over was coming after him. The Greek mob was in Philadelphia, and he wanted in on that area. The Albanians were in New York, and he wanted that area. He wouldn't suspect us because for one, he thought my brother and I didn't have the guts. Second, he set up the MC motorcycle club to take the fall for our brother's death. What he did not know was that my cousin Santos was a member of their club. Santos and the president, Kro Jamison, had been best friends since we were kids.

Volkov had no one else to turn to when this was finished. And next week, our plan would unfold, and I could taste the revenge.

Annika

I was finally Dr. Annika Volkov. I graduated with a 4.0 GPA. My mother would have been so proud of me. She had been the voice in my head all these years, telling me that I could do it.

"I miss you, Mom. I wish you were here."

I made it this far, and I could stop, but I would love to get my residency to be a surgeon. Being a Mafia princess set my limits on what I could do. I was not sure why my father had not married me off yet, but that was my destiny. I thought for so many years of how to get out. How to run and hide. Have my name changed and live my own life. But it was just a dream. I would never be able to change my name as a doctor. My father would always find me.

What if I couldn't work as a doctor? What if my future husband was as bad or worse than my father? What if my father never let me go? Would I try to leave? I would have to make a choice soon. I couldn't keep going on like this. School kept me focused on other things. The reality was I didn't want to live anymore if this was what my life was. I couldn't suffer any more at my father's hands. Hope only took you so far before you gave up. The reality of my life, even without the abuse, was grim. I was supposed to be voiceless, spineless, and an invisible nothing. That should never be a woman's place.

If I was the head of the Russian Mafia, things would be different. Women would have the same rights as men. A right to choose, no matter the choice. I could only imagine all the Mafia women going through the same shame as me. I was so broken that I would never find all the pieces. I wanted children so badly, but I would not bring them into this life as it is. No child of mine would ever suffer the same fate as I had.

Angelino

We were finally setting our plan to action. Along with our cousins, we recruited some of Santos's biker buddies to help us take down Volkov. This was a precise operation, and everything must take place at once. We put a few things in action before today to make sure everything went smoother. Such as the strip club. It was having "electrical difficulties." The club would be shut down for the night due of the power being out. One of the MC men broke in and damaged the main power all the way down to the breaker. They had to have an electrical crew come out and repair all the damage done. That put all the women back at the whorehouse and at one location. Then Rocco and his team of six would make sure the building was clear and burn it to the ground on command.

The restaurant was shut down at this hour of night. Dante would take Lily James from her house and take her to safety, along with her family. Lily James would be none too pleased about her restaurant being leveled to the ground, but we had a plan to get her going at another location on one of our properties.

Snake and Jax from the MC club would clear the bakery and burn it to the ground on command.

Giovanni and Rocco and a team of thirty men, including some of ours and some of the MC club, would secure the warehouse and have the trucks loaded and shipped to one of our secure locations. They would take control of whatever captive they had until they got the answer. Then they would clear the buildings and blow it up with explosives.

Santos and I had a team of thirty to take care of the whorehouse. We'd load up all the women and get them to safety. Then the school would be leveled to the ground.

CYNTHIA SEIDEL

Luca and Rubble from the MC club were manning COMS and the control center. When all the buildings were clear, they would give the order to level every building to the ground.

We all met at the mansion and geared up in full tactical gear with facial hoods and bulletproof vests. Each person had his earpieces to hear their own team, and Luca had control over the ability to speak and hear everyone. We went over the plan, and then each team broke up and went over their plans one more time and checked all the equipment.

We all mounted up and headed to our staging areas before heading into each of our areas. Luca and Rubble set us all in motion when all the cameras were for our viewing only. Luke had full control of the cameras in each location. This was set up a week ago, and we had been watching their every move. Luke and Rubble would be able to tell us where all of Volkov's men were always located.

"We roll out in thirty seconds," Luca said. "Team 1, are you ready?" Luca asked.

"Ready!" Giovanni said.

"Team 2, are you ready?" Luca asked.

"Ready," I said.

"Team 3, are you ready?" asked Luca.

"Ready," Matteo said.

"Team 4, are you ready?" Luca asked.

"Ready," Dante said.

"Team 5, are you ready?" Luca asked.

"Ready," Snake said.

"Let's roll out!" said Luca. "Check in when you get to your staging areas," Luca said to the entire team.

Each team checked in when they got to their staging areas. Rubble switched the cameras to him and Luca. They were the only ones able to see what the cameras were looking at.

"All cameras are ready. Roll out and be safe," Luca told the teams.

They maintained radio silence until needed. Each team arrived at their locations at the same time and put their plans into action.

Giovanni

Rocco and I left the eighteen-wheelers at the staging area so they would not be seen.

"Team 1 made it to our location," I said.

"Ten-four, there are two armed guards at the gate, two more at the front of the building, and two more inside," said Luca.

"Drifter, you're up," I said. Drifter was one of the MC club's men. He was an ex-Army Ranger and a sniper.

"Ten-four," Drifter replied. Within two seconds, both guards at the front gate were dead. "Targets 1 and 2 are down," said Drifter.

"Ten-four. Rocco, cut the fence, and your team will take out the guy on the left. Will do the same with our guy on the right. Go!"

"Ten-four," Rocco said. Rocco cut the fence so his team of ten could get through. He took out the guy from behind with a knife across his throat. At the same time, I came up behind the guard on the right and snapped his neck. "Target two down," said Rocco.

"Target 3 down," I said.

"Ten-four, you have two more inside the building. One guy is sitting on the couch watching TV to your left. The second guy is in the room with no cameras," said Luca.

Rocco opened the door, and his men followed quietly, and my team followed. We left six of our men outside along with Drifter, who was still hiding to keep the building secure. The others spread out as Rocco and I gave hand signals. Rocco would take care of the guy on the couch and then join me in the room with no camera. I took my team and made it toward the room with the captive. Rocco came up behind the guy on the couch and put a bullet in his head.

"Target 5 down," Rocco said. His guys spread out while Rocco headed to help me.

27

We were not sure what we would find in the room, but we had to be prepared for anything. We had to take down the guy in that room before he could call anyone. One man on my team put his hand on the knob and turned it slowly, not to make noise and to be ready to open it when I gave the signal for my team to enter the room. I nodded, and the guy opened the door slowly as I looked in. There was a short hallway and then what looked like to be cells along the left side of the wall. I stepped in quietly. I could hear the guy yelling at someone. The guy was beating the crap out of his captive, and I could hear the person moaning in pain.

"You're a disgusting pig. They will never come for you," said the guy.

I slowly walked down the hall and peered in the first cell. It was empty. I headed to the last cell where the guy was still knocking the hell out of the guy on the floor and yelling obscenities. My team was at my back, and I hand signaled only to shoot the guy in the leg. We wanted to get some information out of him. I advanced slowly and peered into the cell. The guy had his back to us and didn't see or hear my team come in. He was hovering over someone on the floor. There was no bed or mattress or anything except a bucket in the corner of the room. The guy stood up and kicked whoever was on the floor, and I could hear ribs break and a cry of pain.

I took the guy's left knee out with one shot, and he dropped like a rock. He screamed out in pain and reached for his gun, and I shot him in the right arm as he was hollering in excruciating pain. I opened the cell door and told my team to secure the idiot. I made my way over to see who the guy was on the floor. The man on the floor was filthy. He had old, dirty, and torn sweats and hoodie that was pulled over his head. He was facing the wall and had his back to me. I walked around to look at his face because I didn't want to roll him over because of his broken ribs. As I walked around, I told my team driver in my mic that we were clear and head this way so we could load up.

I kneeled and moved the hoodie off the guy's head, and my heart sank in my chest. It was not a man at all. It was a woman. A very small woman. She was emaciated, and her dark hair was covered in dirt and matted with blood. She was moaning in pain.

"Shhh, baby girl. My name is Giovanni, and I'm going to get you out of here." I pushed her long raven hair out of her face to see if I knew who the girl was. Blood and dirt covered her face. She had a large cut on the right side of her head. Both eyes were swollen shut. Her lips were busted. She had another large cut down the right side of her temple, next to her hairline. Her right arm was at a weird angle. She had several deep cuts from a knife, if I had to guess, across her stomach and back. And she had so many bruises on her face that I couldn't even tell what her skin tone was.

"I'm going to pick you up and carry you to safety, but it's going to hurt. I'm sorry for that," I told her as I kissed her forehead. "Control, I'm going to need a doctor at the house ASAP," I said into my mic.

"I'm on it, Giovanni. He will be here when you arrive," Luca said.

"We have most of the trucks loaded, and we will secure this guy and get him into holding. Giovanni, you go ahead and get the girl some help," said Rocco.

I cradled the woman to my chest, and she weighed nothing in my arms. Looking at her like this did something to me, and I wanted to hold her to my chest and never let her go. I wanted to torture every person who ever hurt her. I knew in that moment I would always protect her.

"Thank you. I'll meet you at the mansion," I said to Rocco as he headed to the mansion.

"Team 1 is clear and ready for destructions on control's command," I heard Rocco say as he pulled into the drive of his mansion.

Angelino

At the same time, team 2 were doing their own takedown.

"Team 2 is at the staging area. Trucks will remain back until school is cleared," I spoke.

"Ten-four, cameras are all in our favor. There are four armed guards around the school, two in the back and two in the front. There are two more armed guards in the north part of the building and two more in the south end."

They kept all the women in the north end in the old cafeteria. The room was lined with bunk beds for sleeping, and the wall with vanities for them to get ready for the strip clubs and for their clients. The school was a perfect holding area for the women. It had showers from the old PE area. It had a kitchen area so they could for cook all twenty-seven women. The old classrooms were fitted like luxury suites or high-end hotel rooms. Each had a king-size bed with a strip pole in the middle of the room. There was a bar in the room with whiskey, wine, and a few other liquors. There was a wall with a torture rack and sexual toys. That way, whatever the client wanted, it was on hand. Different clients paid for different things. They got the pick of what girl they wanted. The school also housed women that were going up for auction. They held the auctions in the gym. All bleachers were removed, and they built the stage area, and the floor had several round tables for their potential buyers.

"Ten-four, sniper 1, sniper 2, take out the targets and the front and back in five seconds," I said. In five seconds, the sniper took out all four guards on the building.

"All targets are down," Luca said.

"Ten-four," I said.

I hand signaled for my team of ten to head north and to head south.

"Take out the guards and hold your position," I said.

My team and I moved forward. Two guards were standing at the door of the cafeteria where the women were held. With my silencer on, I shot both guys in the head.

"Two targets are down by the cafeteria. We are in holding position," I said.

Santos's team moved south down the main hall.

"One guard just went in the bathroom to your left," Luca said.

They made their way there, and Santos took the guard down as soon as he came out of the bathroom.

"Guard 7 is down. The last guard is standing in front in one of the classrooms down the next hallway to your left," Luca said.

As they moved down the hall, Santos came around the corner and took the guard by surprise. With one shot to the leg, he took him down but didn't kill him. The guard screamed as his team disarmed him, zip-tied his hands and feet behind his back, and threw him in the truck.

"All guards are down. Let's clear the building," Santos said.

After all guards were down, I met up with Santos to find out what was in the classroom. The rest of the team were securing all the women and loading them up in the trucks and clear in the building. They went through all the closets, any cubbyholes, anything in the entire building to make sure there was no one left inside. In the meantime, Santos and I entered the classroom.

What we found in the middle of the room was a woman with her hands tied above her head and attached to the ceiling. Both legs were tied down at her ankles on the floor, where she was standing in wide stance, completely naked. The position must have hurt to hold for a long period. She looked up at us as we walked in. What I was expecting was her to be crying and hysterical, but she looked pissed.

She is gorgeous, Santos thought to himself. She had thick deep red hair that was wild all over her head, and it came down covering one of her breasts and rested against her stomach. The girl was a head shorter than Santos. She had blue eyes and beautiful lips. What he noticed other than her hair was how muscular she was. Not overly muscular for a woman, but very fit and lean. *Damn*, Santos thought to himself.

As we approached her, she said, "For fuck's sake, more fucking idiots."

I looked at Santos like, WTF. She had a black eye, busted lip, and bruises along her body.

"So you fucktards think you can break me? These fucking idiots have tried and have not been successful. How about you untie me and we can make it fair?" the redhead said.

Santos started laughing and said, "Wow, you're full of fire, little one. But we are not here to bring harm to you. We are here to save you and the other girls."

I walked around the table that was sitting a few feet away and stood in front of her.

"Like he said, we're not here to harm you. We're here to help. I'm going to unchain you, and we will get you and the other girls out of here," I said.

The girl nodded once, and I unchained her hands first. When her arms fell free, she whimpered. She must have been sore from hanging there for so long. I removed the chains from her ankles, and before I knew what was happening, she jumped up and grabbed the chains above her head. She pulled her knees into her chest and power kicked me square in the chest, sending me crashing over the table and onto the floor. I lay there with my mouth open.

"Holy shit, cousin, she kicked your big ass," Santos said with a belly laugh as he bent over laughing so hard. He had tears running down his cheeks. He couldn't catch his breath from laughing so hard. I looked at him in awe. For one, yes, I just I just got my ass handed to me by a chick. But also, my cousin hardly spoke, and he never smiled and especially didn't laugh. Not since he was a kid.

As I laughed, I looked up at the woman. "Well, I guess I did get my ass handed to me." I stood up and picked the table back up.

The woman backed herself up against the wall in a stance that said she was ready for a fight. One of the guys that we brought with us walked around the table like he was going to manhandle her. As the guy reached for her, she swung out her left leg, coming across his face and splattering blood from his mouth.

"I'm in fucking love," Santos said.

I backed up as Santos continued to laugh out loud. Santos pulled his T-shirt over his head and threw it at the girl.

"I'm not stupid enough to get that close to you to hand you this shirt," Santos said. The girl looked like she wanted to laugh.

"I think this one has your name all over it," I said to Santos.

"I got her. You guys get everyone else out. We'll be out shortly," Santos said, looking at the girl. The other guard and I left Santos to handle the girl.

"I'm not fucking going anywhere with you!" the girl said.

"That's where you're wrong. We must get you out of here now. We are not going to hurt you. We'll get you out of here and back to your family," Santos said.

"You can try and take me with you, but the only place I'm going to is out of here by myself."

Santos approached her, knowing he did not have time to do this slowly and make her trust him. It was going to have to be the hard way. She kicked her right leg, and he blocked it. She kicked her left leg, and he blocked it. She went to do a combo punch, and he blocked the leg with one hand, and with the other hand, he grabbed her arm and spun her back into his chest as he bent her over the table to hold her still. She was tough, but she was weak from being here. She tensed up and started shaking when Santos pressed his body to hers.

"I'm not going to hurt you, tiger. I promise. But we don't have time for this." He pulled four plastic cuffs from his belt, secured her hands behind her back, and moved to her ankles. He turned around and put her over his shoulder.

"I'm warning you, if you bite me or continue to scream, I will gag you. When we get outside, I'll do my best to do whatever it takes for you to trust me."

She just laid there over his shoulder and did not move. As soon as he got outside, one of the guards stepped up to take the girl, and she started to fight.

"No, she is going to ride with me," Santos said.

The guard that was securing her door yelled out, "He's coming for you, little redhead! He will find you. He's been waiting for you for two weeks. He will not give you up."

One of the guards came up behind him and hit him on the back of the head with a gun and knocked him out.

"Take him to the basement and secure him. I'll have Dante question him later," I said. "Control, the school is cleared."

Santos shifted the girl around so he was cradling her in his arms, and he slid into the back seat with her in his lap.

"What's your name?" Santos asked.

"Take these fucking cuffs," she huffed.

"I can't do that just yet. I don't need a loose tiger in the vehicle. What would help you trust that we are here to help you other than the cuffs? And I will take care take them off, I promise, when we get to the house," Santos said.

She thought about it for a minute. "I want to talk to my mom. She and my sister must be scared."

Santos pulled his phone out of his pocket. "What's the number, tiger?" he asked.

"I don't remember. It was programmed into my phone, and they broke it when they abducted me."

"What's your name?"

"Rachel Payton."

"Okay, Rachel Payton. Now tell me your mother's name and where you live. I'll have my guy get the number," Santos said.

"Do I look that stupid to you? I would never give you the info that could hurt them."

"Fair enough. I can see why you would be scared. So when were you kidnapped?" Santos asked.

"About three or four weeks ago."

Santos sent off a text to Rubble to look for all women reported missing and match them up and send him a number. Not even five minutes later, he got a reply with a phone number. Santos called the number, and an older woman answered the phone.

"Yes, ma'am, is this Gloria Payton?" Santos asked into the phone.

Rachel's eyes went huge, and they were staring at each other.

"Yes, it is. Who is this?" Gloria asked.

"My name is Santos, and I'm calling about your daughter Rachel."

"Oh god, what happened to my daughter?" she asked.

"She is fine, ma'am. She is sitting here with me. We rescued her from a place tonight, and I'm going to let her speak to you. We will take care of her and get her home soon," he said, handing the phone as he released the cuffs around her wrist.

"Mom?" Rachel asked.

"Oh god, my baby girl, are you okay?" her mother asked.

Santos let them talk, and Rachel looked over at him and asked, "Can my mom call this phone to talk to me?" she asked.

"Absolutely, she can, and you will have a new phone when we get back to the house so you'll always be able to speak with her," Santos said.

Rachel relayed the message back to her mom as Santos released the ankle cuffs while she was talking. She ended the call, and with tears running down her face, she said, "Thank you."

Santos reached over and squeezed her hand and left his hand there. He knew something about this girl. Yes, she was a badass, but she was also broken. He knew her being tough was a mask. She was hiding everything she had been through. She was someone who endured more than she should have, just like he did. He was going to be there for her. This girl might not know it yet, but they needed each other.

"Lights out at the strip club still. All is clear," Matteo said.

"Ten-four," Luca replied.

"All clear at the restaurant. I'm leaving two guys here to finish. Oh, and I'm heading to get the chef into protection," Dante said.

"Ten-four. Her apartment has been quiet since she went inside after work."

"Ten-four, headed that way now, and I'll bring her in for protection," Dante replied.

"One person inside the bakery," Luca said.

"Ten-four," Rank said.

One of the MC guys said, "Entering."

Rank led the way through the bakery and made his way to the office. He kicked the door open with his gun ready. The man sitting behind the desk froze. The other two guys secured him. Rank removed the laptop he was working on and swept the rest of the building.

"Bakery is clear," Rank said.

"Ten-four," control said. "Commence with part B of the plan, teams," Luca said.

They got a 10/4 back from all teams. Multiple fires started at each location, and the warehouse was blown up, leaving only debris in its path. All teams headed back to the mansion.

Dante

I headed to the chef's apartment to explain what was happening and to secure her. I had a sedative ready in case she did not want to come quietly.

"Take out the cameras and jam the calls on the chef's building," I said.

"Ten-four, cameras are down," replied Luca.

I headed up to her apartment on the third floor. There was no security at all. It was about 4:00 a.m. now, and she was going to be scared to see a huge man in her living room at this hour. I took off my hood and put it in my pocket. I knew she would be getting up soon and head to the restaurant. She went in and did the prep work and got ready for deliveries on Tuesdays.

I picked her lock and walked in quietly. The apartment had only one bedroom, and the small kitchen and living room were open. There was a small light on over the stove. I made my way to the corner of the room and sat down in an armchair. I was going to scare the hell out of her either way, but I did not want to do it in her room while she was asleep. I did not want her to think I was going there to rape her. About thirty minutes later, I heard her alarm go off, and she made her way down the hall and into the kitchen to make coffee. I knew she had no neighbors right now. Her unit was the first repaired after a mold issue, and the rest were being worked on. As she turned around to leave the kitchen, I turned the lamp on next to me, revealing I was there.

Lily screamed and backed up. I made no move to get up. I did not want to scare her any more than she already was. She was being bullied enough by the Russians. I raised both hands in front of me to show I was surrendering and came in peace.

"I'm not here to hurt you, Lily. I came to talk."

"You're one of Volkov's men. I've been paying him for protection money and doing what he asked. Why are you here?" Lily asked.

"I'm not with Volkov. I'm a Rossi," I said. Her face went ghost white as she backed up against the bar.

"Your family is more dangerous than the Volkovs. What's going on? What are you doing here?" she asked as tears streamed down her pretty face.

"I'm not going to hurt you, Lily. I promise you. Have a seat and let me tell you what's going on," I said.

She slowly moved forward and sat on the chair across from me.

"Like I said, I'm a Rossi, Dante Rossi, and we are in the middle of taking the Volkov family down. I know they have been making you pay fifty percent of your profits and laundering his dirty money through your restaurant."

"Yes. I'm barely able to keep my people paid and my head above water. But I'm sure you're not here on my behalf. So what can I do for you, Mr. Rossi?"

I smiled at her and said, "You're very wrong, Ms. James. I am here for all of us. What I'm fixing to tell you is not going to be easy. Your restaurant has been burned to the ground."

She gasped. "Oh my god, that was my entire life," she said, crying harder.

"We understand that, Ms. James, and we have a property that will be signed over to you. It's in our territory so the Volkovs can't take from you or use you anymore. If you approve of the property, we will get started on remodeling it, and you will be able to design it however you like. Seeing we burned yours to the ground, we will pay for everything. If the property is not to your liking, then we'll get one that is. We just need you in our territory."

She was shaking, and I just wanted to pick her up and hold her.

"So you burned my restaurant to the ground and you're going to buy me a new one? What's the catch?" she asked.

"There is not a catch for you, Ms. James. We are getting what we want by shutting down his laundering service. It will put Volkov in a bad position for a time. It will also piss him off. He and I will be looking for you. Your restaurant is a five-star, and it would not have an issue starting up anywhere. But we will have to keep you safe until things die down. Right now, I need you to come with me. You can have a room back at the Rossi mansion, or you can stay with me for a while."

"Leave here?" she said.

"Yes. You're not safe without our protection. I promise that we have your best interest at heart, and no one will hurt you. I need you to pack a bag because we need to get out of here."

"What about my family? He's threatening my family. He's going to kill them if I leave."

"We already have your family under our protection. They are safe. Please go pack a bag, Lily. We need to get out of here."

Lily was still shaking. She knew what she wanted didn't matter. Volkov had run her life for the last two years, and now another Mafia family was doing the same thing. So she either did as she was told or die or be raped again.

"I'll go pack a bag," she said as she walked to her bedroom.

That went much better than I thought. I did not have to sedate her.

She was going to walk out of here with me. Why was she not fighting? Was she that scared? She was acting very calm, I thought to myself as she came out of the room with two large bags.

I grabbed them from her and said, "Thank you for not fighting me."

*****

She thought of how huge this guy was. He had tattoos running up his neck. She didn't say anything back to him. She was not fighting because she tried that with Volkov, and they beat and raped her.

Self-preservation, she thought to herself. *At least I was able to cook. That was my haven.*

As soon as they got to the car, Dante said into his mic, "The chef is secure."

Angelino

We all met back at the mansion. Giovanni got the girl he rescued to the medical clinic in the basement for the doctor to look at her. He stayed with her during her exam. She was in bad shape. He kept holding her hand and kept talking to her in a calm voice.

Dante brought in the chef with him, and she stayed by his side. He guided her with his hand on the small of her back. She was trembling being around all these huge men. All the main men met in the game room. The fiery redhead was with Santos.

"Let us get the women we rescued to the safe house. Luca and Rubble will start getting information on them, and Matteo will work with them to get them back to their families. The rest of the women we will set up wherever they want to go and make sure they want to go to college."

"Rachel is going to stay with me until we figure out who is coming for her," Santos said.

"The chef will be staying at my penthouse until we get her set up in our territory and things are lined out after Volkov finds out who is messing with him," Dante said.

Giovanni was in the clinic with the girl we found. I'm sure she would be staying with him until we knew more. Plan A had been completed. Now it was time for phase B.

Annika

I woke up to hollering and furniture being turned over and shattered. I walked to my door and cracked it open. Ivan was downstairs with my father.

"I don't know who's behind the attacks. It's not just the bakery that was burned to the ground. They burned the restaurant, the warehouse, strip clubs, and the school," Ivan said.

My father roared, slamming his fists into the wall. "How do you not know who is behind it? It had to be the Greeks or the Albanians," said Volkov.

"There is no surveillance on them at all. The cameras caught nothing. They did not leave our men alive. They killed them, as far as we can tell," said Ivan.

"The Greeks are weak. They must be allied with someone to pull this off. Meet back here at nine. I need to be alone," my father said.

Vera came up beside me and said, "We need to hide you. If he gets a hold of you while he is this angry, he will kill you."

We both knew what alone meant. He was going to pay me a little visit and take every ounce of anger out on me.

"You might be right. Let's go," I said.

Vera grabbed my arm and took me to her room and put me in the back of her closet, behind some long dresses that were hanging.

"Stay here no matter what," Vera said.

Vera walked out of the closet and closed the door. She crawled in her bed, turned the lamp on, and opened the book she was reading. A few minutes later, Vera could hear someone stomping up the stairs, going toward my room.

41

"Where are you, whore? I know you're in here. It's better to come out now!" he bellowed as he threw things around the room. "Annika, show yourself," he said as he came out of the room. He stopped at Vera's room and opened the door. "Where is she?" he screamed at Vera.

"I don't know, sir. I've not seen her."

"You're lying. You know where she is. There's more than one way to skin a cat," he said as he stomped over to Vera. He grabbed her by the hair and dragged her out of the bed as she hit the floor.

Very did not make a sound. I didn't want Vera to give herself up.

"Hey, whore, I have your precious Vera. Come out, or she will pay in your place," he said.

Everything was quiet. He let go of Vera's hair and backhanded her. She crashed into the nightstand, breaking the lamp. Vera still said nothing.

I knew he hit Vera, and she would suffer for my punishment. I stood up and walked out of the closet. My father looked at me, but I was looking at Vera.

"No, Annika, you shouldn't have. You should have stayed put. I don't care what he does to me," Vera said.

"Shut up, bitch. You'll pay for hiding her!" my father screamed.

He walked over to me, grabbed me by my blond locks, and pulled me through the house.

"We're going to have some fun tonight, you little bitch," he said.

I knew this was going to be a bad night. *Would this be the night he kills me?* I thought as he yanked me so hard that I stumbled and fell to my knees. He yanked me by my hair to my feet, and I screamed as he let go of a fistful of my hair. I fell to the ground. He grabbed another fistful as he yanked me forward to the cell in the basement. He opened the door and shoved me in, closing the door behind him. He backed me into a corner, and I covered my face with my arms. He punched me in the stomach, and I dropped to my knees. He punched me right-handed and knocked me out cold. When I woke up, my hands were chained to the ceiling, and I stood up on my toes to relieve the tension on my arms. I still had a broken wrist and ribs from the last beating, so pulling on the cuff that was secured below my cast only brought me more pain. *They would have to reset it after this*, I thought.

"Oh, so you're awake. What should we do first?" he said.

"What have I ever done to you? Why do you hate me so much?" I asked.

He was not used to me mouthing at him. He smacked me open-handed and busted my lip.

"Because you're just like your mother. Weak and pathetic. She was a whore and slept around after you were born. Well, slept around with Boris, my second-in-command. So I killed him to make your mother suffer. But you suffered too. You cared about the pathetic man. So you see, you're just like her. Why could I not have had a son as an heir instead of a stupid girl? They're only good for fucking," he said as he came up behind me. "Are you going to fight me, or are you going to take it easy?" he said.

"No, just kill me. End this," I said.

"I'll end you when I'm good and ready."

I was ready for this to end, to end all the abuse. He could kill me now, and I would be better off. I did not move, and he came over and released the chain from the ceiling. He pulled me over to the table in the room and secured the chains, making me bend over the table.

"Fine. We'll do it your way," he said.

He grabbed a baton off the wall. It looked like a small bat. He started hitting me with it, starting with the back of my legs. I screamed in pain. He continued beating me across my ass and all the way up to my back. A few blows hit bone and opened, spilling blood. I continued to scream in pain, begging him to stop, but that only fueled him. He reached down and unbuttoned his pants. He raped and sodomized me, leaving me bleeding.

"Well, this has been fun, but I must get back to work. I hope you enjoyed yourself," he said to me as he walked out of the cell, leaving me there.

I just wanted the humiliation and pain to stop. I made up my mind that the next time I had the chance, I would end my life.

*****

Volkov met Ivan in his office at nine the next morning.

"I think we need to align ourselves with another local family. That way, we have help with the Greeks and the Albanians."

"I hate the fucking Italians. But we must make alliances until we get the Greeks' territory in Philadelphia. And then we'll take Chicago from the Italians," said Volkov.

"I like this idea. So what are we giving them for this alliance? Your daughter?"

"No!" Volkov said way too fast. The thing was, he loved torturing his daughter. She belonged to him and always would. She was never going anywhere.

"We will give them ten blocks of our territory and let them have that. Annika is too stupid to be anyone's wife, and no one would want her because she is a whore and lost her virginity to some loser kid when she was fourteen," Volkov said, making out his innocent daughter to be something she wasn't. No man had ever touched her except him. "Let's set up a meeting with the Italians and see if we can make an alliance," said Volkov.

"I'm on it," said Ivan.

Volkov left his daughter in the dungeon for two days in the same place. He went down after two days and released her from the chains. She did not make a move. His breath caught because he did not want her dead. He was obsessed with her. He felt for a pulse, and there was a faint one.

"Doc, I need you here immediately. Something has happened to Annika," said Volkov into the phone.

"I'll be there in five minutes," the doc said.

He carried her down to the clinic a few rooms down. He put her on the bed and threw a cover over her body. The doctor walked in, took her pulse, and looked over at Volkov.

"What happened?"

"She was attacked. We found her across the city like this," Volkov said, lying through his teeth.

The doc pulled the sheet back. He could tell she had been beaten and raped and sodomized. He pulled some blood and did some tests.

"She has severe rectal and vaginal tearing. I'm going to stitch her up. And she will need some blood. She has lost a lot. She has a severe infection. I'm sure it's caused by the rectal trauma. She has 104 fever and will need round-the-clock care until the antibiotics I'm putting in her IV start to work," said the doc.

"Looks like you'll be staying until she comes out of it, won't you?" said Volkov.

"Yes, sir," said the doc.

Angelino

It had been a week since we took down the Russians. The plan was working perfectly. We had a meeting with Volkov.

Luca and Rubble had been hacking into their financials. They took three-fourths of all their money and moved it into one of our accounts that could not be traced. This put Volkov in a bigger need for an alliance. That way, I would get what I wanted.

We were meeting on neutral territory in a public restaurant in one of their party rooms. Volkov and Ivan were ahead and seated at the table with a couple of their goons behind them. We entered with two of our men in front and two in the back. My brother and I stood at the table and greeted the two Russians. Giovanni and I sat.

"You called this meeting. What can I do for you, Volkov?" I said.

"Straight to business. I like that," said Volkov. Ivan was scowling at me for the way I spoke to Volkov.

"We want an alliance with the Rossis. It would be in the best interest of both families to have each other's back. We both have an enemy with the Greeks. They helped the MC club kill your brother, and they are taking down my businesses," Volkov said.

Giovanni and I said nothing to them because we both knew he was the one who killed our brother. But we were not ready for him to know that.

"We can take the Greeks and the MC club down by ourselves. What do you have to offer us that we don't already have?" Giovanni asked.

"Shut your mouth, boy. You're not the don!" Ivan said with gritted teeth. Giovanni laughed out loud.

"You called this meeting, Volkov. I will not sit here and listen to your dog speak to my brother that way. So keep him on a leash," I said.

Ivan jumped up from the table and grabbed his gun, and all four of the Rossi guards pointed theirs.

"Sit down, Ivan." Everyone put their weapons away. "Keep your mouth shut, Ivan. And I'm running this meeting," Volkov said to Ivan. He was pissed but did as he was instructed.

"I am one of the dons, Ivan. Giovanni is one, and so are my five cousins. The Rossis are a united front and hold equal power. We are one, and we will be addressed as such," I said.

Volkov nodded in agreement.

"We have ten blocks in our territory that borders yours. We will give that territory to you. It has several businesses and many opportunities."

I already knew what I wanted, but I had to let this play out. I already heard from one of the guards they tortured how much his daughter meant to him. That was why I assumed she was not married off yet because he didn't want that kind of fate for her. I wanted his daughter so I could break her and then break him by hurting his daughter. She was his only heir, and by marring her, I would get her territory when he died.

"We don't need any more businesses. We have large investments all over the world. I appreciate your offer, and I understand your issue you're having with the Greeks, but that is not enough to serve for an alliance with us," I said.

Volkov nodded in understanding "So what can I give you to secure this alliance?"

I looked down at the table like I was thinking.

"Don't you have a daughter? Angelino, we need heirs anyway," said Giovanni.

Volkov was horrified we wanted to take his daughter from him, his toy. He could not allow this.

"She is not part of the bargaining chip, gentlemen. She has special needs and can't be any use to you, Angelino."

"What kind of special needs? Can she not have children or what? I ask because I am curious now." I knew he called her stupid, but she went to college, so I was not sure what the issue could be.

"I love my daughter dearly, but she has been a huge disappointment. She's not a very smart girl. She was born with some kind of learning issues. She's been in school for years, trying to help her learn and to be educated. She is also unsavory, a whore. She lost her virginity at the age of fourteen and has been with several men since then. But she will be of no use to you like that. Should be an embarrassment," Volkov said.

I was not sure I believed him. "Well, that is unfortunate. Because I need an heir, and that would tie our families together. But her being that damaged, I'm afraid you have nothing else to offer us," I said. My brother and I stood up.

"It was great speaking to you, gentlemen, and I'm sorry we cannot work something out. Have a nice day," Giovanni said as we turned around and walked out.

*****

"We must give them something to make an alliance. Maybe your daughter and more territory since she is damaged," said Ivan.

"Fuck," Volkov said.

How had he gotten himself backed up against the wall? If he gave them more territory and his daughter, he could get them back after they killed the Greeks. He would be stronger and could take down the Italians and get what was his and everything else that belonged to him, he thought to himself,

"Fine. I'll call them and see what they say." They would have to wait a week. Annika was still bruised up badly, and they must remove the stitches. He could make up a story about her being attacked. But he needed to get her back as fast as he could. He could not do without his daughter and his little plaything for long.

Angelino answered his phone, so it picked up on Bluetooth in his SUV.

"What can I do for you, Volkov?" he said.

"Rossi, I know my daughter is damaged, but she was raised to be a meek wife. She can have children, and that is all you need. Your wife does not need to be smart. She just needs to be pretty to show off at parties and to carry your children. And for her not being a virgin and for being damaged, I'll give you more property to make up for it. Just tell me what you want," Volkov said. Volkov kept his daughter on contraceptives that kept her from getting pregnant. It was placed in her arm and was good for five years. She was on year 4, so she was good for another year until he could get her back. She would not be having this idiot's kid.

*****

I looked over at Giovanni. We both smiled because we were getting what we wanted.

"Okay Volkov I'll take your daughter and the properties that sit on lake Michigan, all of them. Three apartment buildings and eight other buildings along the lake that would be a great investment.

"Done," Volkov said. "We can meet in a few days. I will sign the papers over to the properties, and you can meet Annika. And we will start planning the wedding."

"Let me know what day and we'll be there," I said.

The phone went dead. Phase B was coming together beautifully. We both laughed and headed back to the mansion.

Annika

I woke up to our family doctor hovering over me.

"I'm glad to see you're awake," the doc said.

"I'm not. You need to just stop saving me. Just let me die," I said.

"We both know he would kill me if you ever died. He would blame it on me and not himself," the doc said.

"So what's the damage this time?"

"Rectal tearing and a nasty infection from it for being left so long and not being cleaned. I got your fever down and stitched you up. You have several stitches along your back and some in your rectum," he said with sad eyes.

"He is getting more violent each time. My life won't last much longer anyway. How long have I been out this time?" I asked.

"Four days since I got here and probably a day before I got here. You need to eat something. You were too thin before. Now you have lost more weight. I'll go get you something. And you can take your pain meds. You're going to need them," the doc said.

"Did you check my hand to see if it is healing? I think he rebroke it."

"No, I didn't. Let me x-ray it really quick," the doc said.

Sure enough, it was broken and out of line. He was going to have to reset it and recast it.

"I'm sorry, honey, but I'm going to have to reset it. I'm going to have to give you a morphine shot to help with the pain, but it's still going to hurt."

"My entire life is pain. At least you're not doing it intentionally."

I screamed as he reset it. God, this could never go any easier.

50

He made sure I ate, and then he let me rest. I'd be getting back to my horrible life tomorrow, so he let me rest. I slept through the night with the help of the pain medications. The doctor helped me get dressed and helped me up so he could take me to my room. He handed me some pain pills and told me he would be back in a few days to check on me and remove all the stitches.

The few days went by slowly and painfully. Each day got better. I had not seen my father. But I knew I wouldn't. He did this every time he hurt me this severely. He was letting me heal so he could try to kill me later. The doc showed up just like he said he would and removed the stitches in my back and my rectum. I just wanted to die right there as he pulled them out.

"Thanks, Doc, for taking such good care of me all the time," I said as he squeezed my hand.

Vera had been watching me like a hawk so I couldn't end my life.

"Your father has asked to see you in his office," Vera said as she entered my room.

My stomach sunk to my feet like it always did when he wanted to see me.

"Thank you, Vera. I'll head there now," I said. I approached his office and knocked on the door softly.

"Enter," I heard my father say.

"Papa, you wanted to see me?" I said as I entered his office and stood in front of his desk.

He did not get up from his chair. "Sit. There are some things I want to discuss with you," he said.

Annika knew they would not be discussing anything because her father ran her life. He was going to tell her what she was going to do.

"Yes, Papa?"

"I don't tell you anything about my business, but I'm letting you know I made an alliance with the Italians. You are part of that alliance, and you're going to marry Angelino Rossi," my father said. He waited for me to say something, but I knew better.

"Yes, sir," I said without another word.

"Good. We are on the same page. Your loyalty will remain with me, and you'll find out anything you can and report back to me. Am I understood?"

"Yes, sir. I understand."

"Good. Now there is no talk of what happens in this house. And I mean nothing. I will kill Vera if I find out that you have. You fell down the stairs. That's what happened to your face, wrist, anything else that's bruised or broken or cut. Are we clear?"

"Yes, Papa," I said to my father, trying to sound as sincere as possible.

"Get ready. Wear something nice and make yourself up. They will be here in an hour to meet you."

"I'll be ready, Papa." I stood and walked out the door.

I knew of the Italians. They were just as ruthless as my father. Would he beat and rape me too? Or did I have a chance of a better life? I would hold off on ending my life to see how things went with my future husband.

Wow, I'm going to have a husband, I thought. Then my stomach dropped. Why would my father allow me to leave? He always told me he would never let me go. Maybe he needed this alliance badly. He wanted me to spy on my husband's family. I would never do such a thing. I was going to do my best at being a great wife. If he was horrible, I had the same options to consider, I thought as I took a hot bath and got ready. I curled my hair and put some makeup on to cover the bruises. My lip was still red from being split, and I still had a black eye under the makeup. If he looked, he could still see everything, but I covered it as well as possible. I would cover the rest of the bruises and cuts with my clothing. I chose a black knee-length pencil skirt and a V-neck silk sleeveless blouse. It was loose around my breast down to my stomach and then fitted at the bottom. I was very skinny, but I had larger breasts. The V-neck shirt was sexy but did not show off cleavage. The blouse was the color of my lips, a pale pink. I picked out a three-inch pair of black stilettos to go with it. A little jewelry and a splash of my favorite jasmine perfume, and I was ready.

"Your father said his guests are here. He told me to remind you to be on your best behavior. I pray this is a new future for you," Vera said.

"I pray that too, but I'm not getting my hopes up. It's another Mafia family."

I made my way downstairs to my father's office. There were several men outside. Some of them were my father's men, and some of them were the Rossis'. I entered his office.

"Papa, I'm here." I walked over to kiss him on his cheek, acting like the daughter that I was supposed to be. I stood next to my father as the two Rossi men stood as soon as I announced I was there. Both men were huge, not just tall but wide. There were both covered in tattoos. Even in business suits, I could see them poking out of their collars and on their hands. They were both gorgeous with dark hair and dark eyes. They both looked like dark angels. I stood straight like a woman of standing should when all I wanted to do was sink in the hole and hide.

"Annika, these are the Rossis." He pointed to the one standing in front of me. "This is Angelino, your future husband. And this is his brother, Giovanni," my father said.

They both walked up to the desk, and Angelino was the first to extend his hand. I put my hand in his, and it was so big and warm that it felt like home.

"It's very nice to meet you, Angelino." Then I shook Giovanni's hand. "And you, Giovanni."

"We are pleased to meet you too, Annika," both men said.

I stepped back to stand next to my father. I shivered as I thought about my father's words earlier, about us having months together before the wedding. It never got any easier. Every time he touched me, it was like it just happened.

Angelino

We parked in front of the Volkov mansion. We had an SUV in the front and one behind us. All but two of our men walked in the house. The two men stayed outside to make sure nothing was touched on either of our vehicles, like GPS or bombs, things of that sort. One could never be too careful. We made our way down to Volkov's office. We left two of our men outside his office, and two guards came in the office with us. His office was not too big. We entered the office, and his desk was set along the wall to the left. He was seated so he could see whoever entered his office. Volkov greeted us and had one of his guys pour us some vodka.

Does this idiot know that we're Italian? I thought to myself.

"I just sent for Annika. She'll be down shortly. So do you want to sign the property papers and contracts between us now, or would you like to meet my daughter first?"

"I would like to meet your daughter first," I said they handed the contract to the lawyer we brought with us to look over.

"Papa, I'm here," Annika said as she entered the room.

I looked over at the woman to see what I was getting myself into. I was in so much trouble. *This woman is sex on a stick*, I thought to myself. She was way too thin, but she had long curly blond hair, medium breasts, long sexy legs, and those "fuck me" heels she had on. She had the bluest eyes I had ever seen, eyes you could get lost in. She dressed sexy but eloquent. She held herself to a standard of elegance. So this woman was a whore? I couldn't see how she could be. She was gorgeous. I eyed her up and down. I looked over at her father, and his teeth were gritted. He did not like me checking his daughter out. As she stepped up and kissed her father's cheek, I could tell it was forced. *Interesting*, I thought to myself. Her father introduced us. My brother and I stood up and took her hand. As soon as she touched my hand, the energy went straight to my cock. Down, boy. Not here. I looked at her more closely.

She had a black eye and a busted lip. What the fuck?

"How did you get the bruises and busted lip? And what happened to your hand?" I asked. Her father put his arm around her shoulder, and she tensed up.

"I fell down the stairs. I'm sorry, but I am very clumsy," she said.

"I see," I said. She even spoke with elegance.

"I accept Annika as part of the alliance," I told Volkov. "Are the contracts in order?" I asked my lawyer.

"They are, sir, to everything you agreed to."

"Annika, this marriage is something you want?" I asked.

"Yes, sir," she said too fast.

"Very well. Let's get these papers signed," I said.

"Annika, you can head back upstairs," her father told her.

"No, I want her here. She is part of this contract. I want her to hear the terms," I said to Volkov, and he was pissed. They didn't want their women to have anything to do with their business, and he sure didn't want her to know the terms.

"Very well," Volkov said.

My lawyer started reading off the terms of the contract. I watched Annika's face as they read the terms.

"On top of the ten blocks that adjoin your current properties, you'll get Annika Volkov as your wife, but due to her being damaged goods, you'll get the eleven properties on Lake Michigan." He listed off all the property addresses.

Annika started shaking. She looked pale. Her father dug his fingers into her shoulders so hard I thought she might scream. She feared her father.

"Annika, you know what damaged goods means?" I asked her, wanting this to hurt them both because this was my plan.

"Yes, sir. It means I'm not a virgin," she said with tears in her eyes. She looked so fragile standing there, so small.

I just wanted to hold her. I could see the pain in her eyes. *Get it together, man. You're here to break her and her father. Stop catching feelings,* I thought to myself.

"Yes, and for the several other men you've slept with and for not being very intelligent, we are being compensated by your father. Do you understand?"

The tears fell down her cheeks, and my heart broke for her.

"Yes, sir. I'm very sorry I'm so damaged," she said with a sob. She didn't even deny it.

But I wanted to smack the smirk off her father's face. He was loving her humiliation. What kind of man and father did that to his daughter?

"Come here, Annika," I said.

She stepped away from her father and came over and stood in front of me with her head down, looking at her feet. She was trembling. I was going to break this girl. What I was afraid of was she was already broken. Her father did not want me to have her. But I think he had been abusing her. She looked so defeated. I put my finger under her chin and made her look at me. Those big blue eyes landed on me and just sunk my heart. I brushed my thumb along her jaw.

"All the contracts are signed. Now just the marriage is left, and you'll have your alliance," I said, looking at Volkov over his daughter's head.

"You can head upstairs, Annika. I'll be up later, and we will start planning the wedding," Volkov said to his daughter. She tensed up and then started shaking again. I pulled her to my chest.

"No, she is coming with me now. We will figure out the wedding in a few days," I told Volkov.

"That's not what we agreed on. She stays here until the wedding."

I started laughing as I held his trembling daughter. "I don't think so, Volkov. She is mine as of now, and if truth be told, I don't think she really wants to be here with you," I said to Volkov. He stared at me but said nothing. "I'll contact you about the wedding. Have a great day."

Giovanni stood in front of Annika and my lawyer, and the guards followed us. We walked to the hall, and Annika stopped and looked at me.

"What is it?" I asked her.

"I don't deserve to ask you this, but can I bring my housekeeper, Vera, with us? He will kill her if I leave her," Annika said, trembling.

Vera was standing by the staircase, staring at us.

"Of course, but we need to leave now. I'll get you what you need when we get to our house," I said.

"Thank you, sir," she said with her head down.

What was this broken woman doing to me? One of the guards ushered Vera to the car with me and Annika. She was still shaking.

"We do not hit women in my family. You don't have to be scared," I told her.

Vera looked at her and smiled. "You're going be okay, Annika." Such mothering words. Words for a wounded child.

Annika was no child, but she sure seemed wounded. How in the hell could I ever add to this girl's pain? She was already in pieces. I was going to have to come up with another plan.

As we sat in the car and headed back to our mansion, I looked at Annika.

"You'll have your own room, and we will consummate our marriage when we know each other better and you're comfortable."

She seemed to relax after I said that. Why would a whore be worried about having sex if she had done it several times?

"Vera, what did you do for Volkov?" I asked her.

"I took care of Annika's needs," she said.

"Is that something you would like to continue to do, or is there something else you would prefer?" I asked.

"I would like to continue taking care of Annika, if I could please."

"Very well. There is a room next to hers if you want to take that," I said.

"Oh, yes. Thank you, sir."

I was not sure what was going on with Annika, but I must find out and make a new plan. There was something about this woman.

I did not want to hurt her. She was not the Russian princess I was expecting.

"I'm sorry we left all your things. As my future wife and partner, you'll have access to everything that is mine. After we marry, it will be ours. I'll have you added to the accounts, and you can go shopping and get whatever you need or want. Same goes for your rooms. Make yourself comfortable."

I was putting her on my personal accounts for now but did not trust her enough until her father was dead to add her to everything.

"Really? You would let me go out and shop and get whatever I want?" Annika asked me. She sounded really surprised.

"Yes, I want you to be comfortable." What I didn't want to say was I wanted to spoil her and make her happy. "I'll add you to my accounts when I get home. You can use my cards until yours come in. But you'll have four guards with you when you're outside the house," I told her.

"I understand. Thank you very much," she said with a smile.

Wow, I thought to myself. *She looks generally grateful and thankful. I guess I will have to see how much of my account she blows through this afternoon.*

"Annika, do you have a phone?" I asked her.

"Yes, but it only has my father's number in it. It won't let me call anyone else," she said.

"I'm going to throw your phone out and get you a new one. You can give your father your number and whoever else you want," I told her.

She took her phone out of her purse she had across her body without hesitation and handed it to me. I dropped it in glass of wine that was sitting in the holder. "I'll throw it out after it gets a good soak," I said to her as I gave her a wink. She gave me another small smile and blushed.

"Vera, do you have a phone?" I asked.

"No, sir."

"Okay, good. Annika, I would like to have you looked at by our doctor and make sure you're okay."

She tensed up like she was scared. What the hell was going on?

I picked her hand up and put it between mine.

"I just want them to check you out. I will not allow them to do anything you don't want them to," I told her. She looked at me with tears in those big blue eyes.

"Thank you," she said as she looked down at our hands.

We pulled through the gates into the circle driving in front of the mansion. Annika's eyes were huge as she looked at the place.

"It's gorgeous," she said.

"Thank you. It used to be an old castle. It's been in our family for years. Giovanni, I'll meet you later. I want to get the ladies settled," I said.

Annika

When he allowed me to stay in the office for the contract sign-ing, I felt empowered. Until they started reading the terms. Then I realized what my father told him. That I was a whore. My heart sunk at the mention of it. Angelino thought I was a whore. My future husband would always look at me like I was trash. And he told him I was an idiot on top of it. How desperate was my father? How could he continue to break me? Every man in this room thought I was a stupid whore. My father's fingernails dug into my shoulder to remind me to keep my mouth shut.

"You know what damaged means, right?" Angelino asked me.

"Yes, sir. It means no longer a virgin," I told him.

"Yes, and for the several other men you slept with and for not being very intelligent, we are being compensated. Do you under-stand?" he asked me.

The tears rolled down my cheeks. How could one person hate themselves so much? And I did in that moment.

"Yes, sir. I'm very sorry I'm so damaged," I said with a sob with my head down, looking at the floor.

"Come here, Annika," Angelino said.

Was he going to hit me or something worse in front of every-one? I stepped away from my father and walked up to Angelino with my head down. *Please, no more shame. Please,* I thought to myself. I was shaking so bad I couldn't control it. He lifted my chin, so I was looking into his beautiful brown eyes. They were not filled with mal-ice but what looked like sorrow. He stroked his thumb over my jaw in a kind way. No one had ever touched me like I was precious. *Why is he doing this?* I thought to myself. *I don't understand.* He looked over my head at my father.

"All the contracts are signed. Soon as we are married, you'll have your alliance," Angelino said to my father.

"You can head upstairs, Annika. I'll be up later, and we will start planning the wedding," my father said to me.

Oh god, I know what that meant. More rape and beating. He was warning me about what he was going to do to me later. I started shaking. I started to back up, but Angelino pulled me to his chest in a protective manner. He had his left arm wrapped around my back, securing me in place. God, he smelled so good. Like spice and whiskey. He smelled like comfort and home. It felt so good for him to hold me.

"No, she is coming home with me now. We'll figure the wedding out later," Angelino said to my father.

He was taking me now. *Does he sense something, or does he have some ulterior motives?* I thought to myself.

"That is not what we agreed on. She stays here until the wedding," my father said.

Oh god, please, no. Angelino started laughing, and I could feel the rumble in his chest.

"I don't think so, Volkov. She is mine as of now. And truth be known, I don't think she wants to be here with you," Angelino told my father.

Oh my god, no one had ever spoken to my father like that. How did he know? How did he know I did not want to be here?

"I'll contact you about the wedding. Have a great day," Angelino said.

My father did not say a word. Angelino's brother stepped in front of me, and Angelino was at my back in a protective formation. We walked out of the office, and I could see Vera standing at the bottom of the staircase at the end of the hall. He would kill her if she stayed here. How could I ask him to help me? I must do something. I must try. I stopped and turned around and looked at him.

"What is it?" he asked.

"I...I don't deserve to ask you this, but can we bring my house-keeper, Vera, with us please? If I don't, he will kill her," I said as I pointed at Vera.

"Of course," he said. "But we must leave now. I'll get you whatever you need when we get back to my place," he said.

"Thank you, sir," I said to him.

I felt overwhelmed that we were getting out of here. I was scared of what the future held, but it could not be any worse than the hell I had been through. On the ride to the house, he took my phone and told me he would get me a new one that I could use anywhere. And he would set me up on his bank accounts so I could get whatever I needed and wanted. Shopping? I had never done that in my life. I was allowed to go outside if I had security, he told me.

We pulled up to his house slash castle because that was what it was. It was the biggest property I had ever seen. Something from a fairy tale.

Angelino walked us through the mansion and showed us where everything was. He introduced us to his cousin Luca.

"Luca, this is Vera and my soon-to-be wife, Annika. They both need phones with tracking and access to security. I need them monitored so we know that her father does not use her to get into the house," he said.

I flinched, and he saw it.

"It's not because of you, Annika. Your father is still a threat, and I won't have him using you to get access to the house. Do you understand?"

"Yes, I do."

I did, but it still bothered me. *Don't trust the Russian whore.*

"Also, every person who works for us or are related to the Rossi family have tracking chips inserted in their bodies. It's not a choice. We all have one. Luca, if you can get two ready, and you can bring them up to their rooms," Angelino said to Luca.

These people took security to a whole new level.

"Yes, I'll bring them up, along with two new phones. I'll go over the security system with you ladies tomorrow," Luca said to us.

"Thank you, Luca," I said and followed Angelino to his wing of the house.

The place was dark, but I was here as a guest and nothing more. I was sure they would not appreciate me opening the blinds to let in some light.

"This is my wing of the house. Both of you will have your own rooms and can come and go as you please."

"Here's your room, Annika. And, Vera, yours is on the other side. Mine is at the very end if you need anything. I'm going to let you look around a bit, and I would like to have a conversation with you about our wedding a little later if you're up to it, Annika."

"Yes, that would be great. Thank you," I said.

"So make a list of everything you need, and I'll have my driver take you out later to go shopping. I'm going to add you to my accounts now. Ask anyone if you can't find me, and they will direct you to me. I know this house is overwhelming. I'm happy you're here, Annika," he said.

I knew I blushed. I could feel the heat. This guy couldn't be real. What was he plotting? Maybe he was not horrible.

I walked into the room. It was huge, three times as big as my room in my father's house. It had a huge dark canopy bed against one wall that had windows that were covered in drapes. I walked over and pulled them open. They were doors that went out on the huge balcony overlooking Lake Michigan. I wanted to cry. It was so beautiful. There was no seating out here, and that was a shame. I left the doors open to let the fresh air in and light. There was a huge fireplace to the left of the bed. But there was no couch or chair or anything to sit on. A reading nook or something on the far wall would be amazing. I walked through a large open door on the wall where the fireplace was, and there was a huge bathroom with a double tub with no shower. And the tub looked out over the lake. It also had a fireplace on the same wall as the fireplace that was in the living room.

The floors were all stone, and the counters were also the same stone or rock with two sinks in one huge mirror, about fifteen feet. This would be awesome as a vanity. I walked to the glass double doors to the back and opened them. It was a closet the size of my old room.

"Holy shit," I said to myself. There was a simple light above. But the room was twenty feet wide like the bathroom and just as long. It had places for shoes and clothes galore. I never had a lot of clothes. My father made sure I had a new dress if he had an event. But I did not get to go to many of those. A couple in my lifetime overall. I could walk gracefully in heels. I was taught as part of my grooming. I only owned about three pairs. This place was amazing. This room needed a chandelier and a large chaise to put on my shoes with a couple floor-length mirrors.

I walked over to Vera's room. It was not as big as mine. But at the old house, Vera stayed at the back of the property and shared quarters with the rest of the help. This room had a fireplace and a door with a balcony also. Her bathroom had a walk-in shower and a smaller walk-in. Yet it was still bigger than her old room. We wrote down everything we would like to have and things we needed. I already knew I would not get a lot, just enough to get by. That's just who I was. I did not want to take Angelino for granted.

Angelino

"Hey, brother," Giovanni said when he entered the room.

"What's wrong? You have that look on your face," I said to my brother.

"I found out who the girl is."

"Okay. Then you should be happy. You've been so wrapped up and concerned about her."

"I am happy she is healing and that she was not raped," he said to me.

"Then what the hell is the problem?"

"Amelia Argyros."

I just stared at him. "Wait, you mean as in Apollo Argyros's daughter?"

"The same one. She said the Russians kidnapped her to make her father give up his territory in Philadelphia by marrying her when she turned twenty-one. She said Volkov told her that he could not marry her until she turned twenty-one. He had an agreement with someone. She has been a captive for almost a year and a half and has been abused every day of that."

I just shook my head in disgust.

"Now we know why he wanted an alliance so bad. The Greeks are coming for his head as soon as they find out. I say we use this to our advantage. I don't want Argyros as our enemy. We talk to him and let him know of our plans to take out the Russians. We will give his daughter back and let him know we saved her," I said to my brother.

"No!" said Giovanni way too fast.

I looked over at my brother. "Okay, what are you thinking then?"

Giovanni looked down at his feet and let out a huge breath. "I want to marry her," he said exhaustively.

"How does she feel about it?"

"I have not asked her yet, but she has feelings too. She needs me, brother, but I also need her. She instills a peace in me that I have never had," Giovanni explained.

"Then I think we need to contact him immediately after you speak with your girl. Explain to him that we rescued her from the Russians, and she just now told us who she was. Have him come here, or we can go there with her for a family reunion. If she agrees, then you marry her. And if she does not agree, we have to set her free."

"I agree. I don't want her against her will. What if her father will not allow it?"

"We don't give him a choice. We will ask his permission, and if he denies it, then we will go to war for your girl. We'll take him out first, and then the Russians," I said to my brother.

My brother looked relieved at my words.

"Okay. Thank you, brother. I'm going to go speak to her now. I'll let you know what she says." Giovanna got up and left.

This was going better than I planned. My brother was in love.

I met up with Luca and headed up to the girls' room. I found them in Annika's room, walking around and discussing what should go where, a list in her hand.

This is going to cost me a pretty penny, I thought to myself. Not that it mattered. I was worth billions. It was just the fact that she must be used to all of this.

"Hello, ladies," I said as I entered.

Annika immediately dropped her head and said hello.

"So here are your phones. My number and Luca's number are programmed in. I will give you the rest of the Rossi cousins' numbers, the guards, and your drivers' numbers."

"Thank you very much, Mr. Rossi. This means so much," Annika said to me.

"Call me Angelino, Annika. We are going to be married soon," I said to this beautiful girl in front of me. She blushed.

"Okay, Angelino."

My name never sounded so good on a pair of lips.

"How do you like your room, Annika?"

"I love it. It is stunning with a stunning view."

Not as a stunning as you, I thought to myself.

"I see you have a list started to purchase what's needed."

"They're just ideas I had," she said shyly.

"Here are my bank cards. Your name is added on. They will send you your own cards in a few days. When we are finished here, I'll have the driver take you shopping. You get whatever you need or want. The stores know who I am and will deliver anything here."

Annika looked at me in disbelief, like she had never had such a gift.

"Thank you very much. We both appreciate it more than you could know."

"You're welcome. Now we need to insert you with the trackers. They are small, but they need to be in a fleshy and fatty part of a body," I said to both ladies.

Annika started breathing erratically, and then she started shaking. Vera walked over to her and whispered in her ear. She was shaking her head no. I walked over to her and put her hand in mine, and she looked up at me.

"What's wrong, Bella?" I asked her calmly.

She did not say anything. She just stood there, shaking. I pulled her to my chest and wrapped my arms around her. God, she felt so good.

"There's nothing to be afraid of, Bella. This is for your own protection so we can find you if something happens to you. It may sting a little, but I will never hurt you or let anyone else hurt you."

Her breathing steadied, and she started to calm down a little.

"Look, I'll get another one. If it makes you feel better, you can watch me get it," I said to her.

She looked up at me and giggled a little. God, that giggle did me in. No way in hell I could not take this marriage to her seriously. I couldn't stand the thought of someone hurting her.

"Are you okay now to have this done?" I asked her.

"Look, I'm going get mine now," Vera said. She was a heavy woman and could get hers anywhere. We put it on the underside of her arm.

"It pinched a little, but I'm fine," she told Annika, trying to reassure her.

*****

That wasn't the biggest issue she had. She knew they would see her ugly skinny body and see all the bruising and the things that she had been through. What if he found her hideous and did not want to marry her? What if he sent her back to her father? Tears started running down her eyes before she could stop them, and she had a hard time catching her breath.

*****

I pulled her into me again and held her tight.

"Easy...it's okay. Tell me what got you so upset, Bella. Let me understand this. Can you all step out and let me talk to Annika? Leave the syringe here please, Luca."

I picked her up and carried her to the bed and sat upright against the headboard, still holding her.

"I'm going to be your husband. Talk to me, please," I whispered to her.

*****

She knew he would see her body eventually. And it shook her to her core. She had seen her body every day and knew what it looked like. It was nothing to be cherished.

*****

"My body is...is ugly. I don't want you to be disgusted," she said with tears streaming down her face.

"There is not an inch on you I would find disgusting ever. Do you even know what *bella* means?" I asked her.

She shook her head no.

"It means beautiful. Because you are. Even your gentle spirit is beautiful."

She looked up in my big brown eyes, and she could only see the truth.

"Thank you for that. It means more to me than you'll ever know," she said quietly.

"I'm not going make you get the chip if you're still scared. I don't want you upset again. I'll have to find another way to protect you."

"It's okay. I'll have it done. But can you please do it? I don't want anyone else to see my body," she asked me.

"Of course. I don't want anyone else looking at your body either. And after I do this, will you have dinner with me on the terrace after you get back from shopping? We have a great chef."

"I would love to," she said with her head down, looking at her lap.

"Okay, let's get this over with then and get on to the good stuff," I said with a little bit of a chuckle.

I picked her up and set her on her feet.

"It needs to be in some kind of fat. You don't really have a lot on your body, but I think your butt is going to be the best place to insert it. Are you okay with that? I'll only pull your skirt down enough for the shot," I said to her.

She took a deep breath and then exhaled it. "Yes, I'll be okay."

Grabbing the shot off the bed, I told her, "Turn around. I'm going unzip your skirt and give you the shot and zip you back up. Are you okay with that?"

She was still nervous. It was rolling off her in waves.

"Here we go," I said to her as I unzipped her skirt until it was low enough to flip over her cheek.

She was breathing a little heavier than she should be, but she said, "Yes, I'm okay."

"I need to pull your panties down enough to give you the shot. Are you good with that?"

"Yes."

I inserted the shot as quickly as I could. This wasn't even sexual, not because she wasn't gorgeous but because she was so scared. As soon as I pulled her panties down over her left cheek, I saw the fresh bruising and some scarring, and it pissed me off. I stood up and pressed my body against hers and set my chin on her shoulder.

"You did great. You are so brave, Bella. And so gorgeous. I would really like to lift your shirt up and look at your back," I asked her. "I see some bruising under your shirt and want to see how bad it is." She froze in place and stiffened. "I'll never hurt you ever. And you're gorgeous. I know your father has been abusing you. I just want to see the damage and see if I need to have a doctor called in to look at you." She started to relax.

"Okay, you can."

I lifted her shirt up past her bra, and what I saw fucking angered me. She was scarred all the way down her back. She had recently healed stitches that had been removed, and she was so thin that every bone she had was protruding. This girl was starved. I kissed her back in several places and brought her shirt back down and then kissed the back of her head. I turned her around and wrapped my arms around her.

"You're so brave, Bella. When you're ready to talk to me about what happened, I'm here for you. I will always protect you. You're safe here, and you're safe with me." She fisted the back of my shirt and sobbed.

"Thank you," she said in a whisper.

"You have stiches that need to be removed. I'll take care of it for you later."

I kissed her again on the head. No way in hell I would ever be able to hurt this girl. She had been tortured, and I was going to do my best to take care of her and give her a better life.

"Do you feel up to going out and get the things you need, or do you want me to wait? And we'll have dinner about seven on the terrace. Just you and me. We will discuss the wedding, and there is something I would like to tell you."

"Yes, I would like to go pick up some things, if you're okay with that," she said as she looked at the floor.

"Let me text my guards and your driver. I'll walk you downstairs and to the door so you don't get lost," I said with a chuckle.

She smiled. "Thank you," she said so shyly.

I would tell her about my daughter tonight and let them meet tomorrow. I wanted to them to get used to each other before my controlling mother came back from Italy. She had been gone there for months, visiting her sister. She was a horrible woman. She was as bad as my father. She was abusive and neglectful all the years of our lives. We allowed her to stay around because she was our mother. But it was horrible to have her around.

I walked Annika and Vera to the car and kissed her on her forehead, making sure she got in the car safely.

Looking at all four guards, I said, "Protect her with your life. Are we clear?"

"Yes, sir," the guards said in return.

"Have fun. I'll see you tonight," I said to her as I shut the door of the car.

Annika

"What happened in the room when we left?" Vera asked.

"He was kind and gentle and made me feel beautiful. How can a Mafia man be any of those things?" I said.

"I just think you were raised in the wrong Mafia family. You, out of everyone, deserve happiness. You deserve to be loved and cared for. Maybe he will even let you get your residency."

"I don't want to ask him right now. I would feel like I'm taking advantage of him. I don't want to do that. He's just been so kind, and I'm just so happy with that."

"He seems to generally care for you. He saved you from your father, and he is still letting you take his cards and go shopping. I say you enjoy yourself."

"I'll try. We are having dinner tonight on the terrace. I need to get a nice dress and some shoes."

"Oh my god, that is going be so much fun. We'll have to pick out something pretty that goes with your long blond hair. What else are we going to pick out today?"

"I just think we get a few outfits each. I'm not comfortable spending his money. I don't want him to think I'm using him. He's just been so good to me all day. And I'm just scared I'm going to upset him and he'll stop being kind."

"I understand, but I think he would never be ugly to you."

We stopped at a couple of high-end stores. Vera got some everyday clothes. I picked out a couple of nice dresses and a couple of sexy stilettos. I picked out three other everyday dresses with a pair of flats. We both picked up underwear, bras, and bathroom stuff. I picked up a few bottles of perfume at another store and a little bit of makeup, and then we headed back to the house.

72

I texted, "I'm on my way back. Thank you for everything."

Angelino texted, "You're very welcome. I hope you got what you needed and you had fun."

I texted, "I did have fun. Now I have shampoo, so my hair does not stink. Lol."

Angelino replied, "Lol, I'm glad to hear that since I kiss your head all the time. I'll see you in a couple of hours, Bella."

*****

He loved that she texted him. She was already getting comfortable with him.

*****

I made it back to the house, and I asked one of the guards to lead us back to our rooms. I didn't want to get lost and be where I shouldn't be. It was about 2:00 p.m. I made it to my room, and I thanked the guard before he left. I went to the closet and bathroom and put all the stuff away. There was a soft knock at the door. I walked over and answered the door, and there was an older lady standing there with a tray of food in her hand.

"Mr. Rossi wanted to make sure you ate," the servant said.

She walked in and set the tray on the bed and walked out. He wanted to make sure I ate. Wow, it was a cheeseburger and fries. No salad, lettuce crap. He was feeding me. I did not hesitate. I kneeled in front of the bed and put the burger to my lips, and I took the biggest bite I could and moaned as the taste hit my tongue.

"Oh my god," I said with a full mouth. I never tasted anything so good in my entire life. I ate half the burger and half the fries. I was the fullest I had ever been. "What if I can't eat dinner? Would he be mad?"

I was so exhausted. I set my alarm on my phone and lay down. I was full and safe and was asleep in seconds.

Angelino

I spoke to the chef and made sure she cooked three meals a day for Annika and had it taken to her. I would speak with Vera and let her know the same thing and that my expectations were for Annika to be fed at least three times a day. I was going to make sure she put weight on.

I had not seen anyone bring in a bunch of bags or any kind of furniture. I'd have to ask her what she bought.

I made my way to the terrace for dinner in a pair of jeans and a button-up shirt. It was blue to match her eyes. I sat down and poured us both a glass of red wine. I looked up as she walked onto the terrace on the main floor. She was dressed in a blue dress that fell to her knees with high-heeled sandals.

Fuck, she is drop-dead gorgeous, I thought to myself. I stood and made my way to her chair and pulled it out for her. I helped her scoot up to the table.

"You look stunning, Bella." She blushed and put her hands in her lap.

"You're very handsome. I love seeing you in jeans." And she blushed again.

How the hell could this girl could be a whore? She wouldn't let anyone touch her, and she blushed at everything.

"Did you eat the lunch I had set up for you?"

"Oh, yes, it was so good. I could only eat half of it, but it was the best thing I have ever eaten."

How is that possible? I thought to myself.

"I'm glad you enjoyed it."

"Thank you. It was incredible. I even took a nap after." She giggled.

Oh god, I loved that sound so much.

"I poured you a glass of red wine. Do you like wine?"

"I've actually never had any. My father does not allow me to drink."

Or eat, I think to himself.

"Well, take a sip and tell me if you like it. If you don't, I'll get you whatever you want."

She brought the glass to her lips and took a sip. God, how I wished it was my lips instead of that glass.

"This is really good. Thank you."

"Great, so we'll discuss the wedding, but I need to tell you something. I have a five-year-old daughter. Her mother left her with me five years ago, but she is my entire world."

"What's her name?"

"Grazia. She means absolutely everything to me and has been my life since the day she was put in my arms."

Annika put her hand over her heart and looked shocked. And she had tears in her eyes.

"What's wrong?"

"Nothing. It's just that I know *Grazia* means grace."

"Yes, it does."

She looked at me and said, "Well, so does *Annika*. We have the same name."

I looked at her in disbelief for a minute. I did not know what her name meant. But what a coincidence. How was that even possible? Meeting a woman that meant the same thing in another language?

"Really? Grazia is going to love that. Both my girls with the same name."

She smiled at me with approval and took another part of my heart.

"When do I get to meet the amazing Grazia?" she asked.

"I would like you to meet her tomorrow. That way, you two can get acquainted. I'm sure she will talk your head off when she knows I'm going to marry you." We laughed.

"Well, I look forward to it."

"You're okay marrying a man that has a child?"

"Absolutely. I would love to be able to have her here to talk to, if that's okay. I have been alone for so long."

Her words broke my heart.

"I would love nothing more."

"Now the wedding of the year, an Italian don and a Russian princess. We will be the talk of the town." We both started laughing.

"Tell me what you want for a wedding."

"I…I don't know," she said, stuttering.

"It's okay, Bella. You can tell me your thoughts. There are no wrong answers here. I'm here to listen."

She let out a breath she did not know she was holding. "I don't want to go back to my father's ever," she said in very small voice with her head down.

"You never will then. What are you trying to say? You want to get married soon?"

"Yes, please," she said as she looked up at me with those big blue gleaming eyes.

"We can do that," I said. "Do you want a big wedding?"

"What do you want?" she asked, which took me off guard. She was asking because she wanted to please me, not thinking of herself.

"It does not matter to me. I just want to marry you."

"I feel the same. Something small with just your family?"

"How about the day after tomorrow here on the beach?" I suggested.

"That would be the perfect wedding. Grazia can be my maid of honor," she said. I started laughing.

"Yeah, if you can get her to hold still long enough." We both laughed out loud. "Grazia was born prematurely. She has some learning disabilities and some issues with her kidneys."

"Is she going to be okay?" she asked sincerely.

"Yes. Her mother was on cocaine when she was pregnant, so it caused her some issues. But she is strong, and she will be fine."

We sat in silence for a few minutes.

"Well, I guess I need to get a dress for the wedding, if you're okay with that?"

"Of course. Anything you want. I didn't see any furniture or bags being moved in. What did you ladies get?"

"I got about seven dresses and a few pairs of shoes. Toiletries and underwear and some bras and a couple pairs of pj's. Thank you again for everything."

"That's all you got? I thought you and Vera had a list?"

"We did have a list. It was just me daydreaming about things."

"Daydreaming? Are they not things you wanted?" The girl spent a few $1,000, and that was it. She didn't go to any high-end stores. I was told by my guards.

"Of course, I want things, but I didn't need any of it. I'm used to making do with what I have. I'm not going to take advantage of you being so kind to me," she said as she looked down at her lap.

I looked at her, dumbfounded. I was still staring at her when they brought our steaks out with the side of asparagus. This girl couldn't be real. *Her father had all the money, and she was used to making do?* I thought to myself. And not take advantage of me. That's all what all the women had ever done and wanted from me. I was a way for them to be rich and powerful. And my little Bella was none of those things.

"Tomorrow, after you meet my daughter, I will take you out shopping. We are getting everything on your list and more," I said in a stern voice, probably a little too stern, making her wince.

"Are you upset with me?" she asked nervously.

"No way, Bella. I'm sorry I came across like that. It's just that you deserve everything I can give you. I want to take care of you," I said as I reached out and covered her tiny hand with mine.

She had tears in her eyes when she said, "Thank you, Angelino."

Oh my god, her saying my name went straight to my heart and down to my dick. *Easy, boy. She has been broken. We must put her back together before you touch her.*

"You're very welcome, Bella. Now let's eat. I hope you like steak. I had them cook it medium rare. I hope that's good."

"That's perfect." She cut into her steak and took a bite. She moaned the seductive, sexy ass moan from a bite of steak.

This woman was going to fucking kill me. She looked up and noticed I was staring.

"I'm sorry. I didn't mean to distract you. It's just good. I think this is now the best thing I've ever eaten," she said with a blush.

I laughed. "You can moan over your food anytime you want to. I love seeing and hearing you enjoy your food." She smiled at me happily.

"What did a typical meal look like at your dad's house?"

She froze in place and looked up with fear in her eyes. And she acted like she was not sure what to say.

"Annika, we are speaking freely here. You can tell me anything at any time, and I will never judge you. This is your home and your safe place. No one can touch you here."

She took a sip of her wine and took a deep breath.

"It was usually a salad with no meat on the days I was allowed to eat," she said, matter-of-fact.

She put another piece of steak in her mouth.

"I'm sorry for all the hell that he put you through. And thank you for sharing that with me. Here, they will cook three meals a day and whatever you want at any time. If you're hungry at 2:00 a.m., call me and I will wake the chef up to make sure he feeds you."

"I might do that. But you might make me fat if I eat all the time."

"You would still be my Bella." She smiled and finished her entire steak and all the asparagus.

The chef brought out a huge piece of German chocolate cake, which we shared. It's like she had experienced everything for the first time.

"I'm so full," she said.

"I must agree with you on that. Would you like a cup of coffee or hot tea?"

"Oh, I would love some hot decaf tea if you have, if it's not too much trouble."

I told the server to bring two.

"You know you can speak without me asking you questions. You can talk about anything or ask me anything."

She looked down at her plate like she was thinking for a minute. Then she looked up with her big blues. "Why do you want this alliance? Why do you want to marry me?"

Shit, I didn't want to lie to her. "The truth is, I want your father dead. He murdered my brother. I was going to marry you to hurt him. But when I saw you today and how scared and hurt you were, I knew I couldn't use you like that. I want to protect you."

"Do you think you will ever change your mind about me?" she asked, unsure of herself.

"No, I don't. I've been around a lot of women, and you're nothing like them. I knew the moment I saw you standing next to your father with tears running down your face that you were mine."

"When I saw you, it reminded me of a dark angel," she said, making me laugh.

"I'm no angel, but I am very dark."

"You're my angel. You saved me." She looked in my eyes and then down at the table.

That took another chunk out of my heart.

"Can I ask you a few questions that may make you uncomfortable?"

"Yes. Anything."

"Why did your father call you stupid? Because so far, I don't see anything that confirms that."

"I have dyslexia. When I read, the words get jumbled up. I've learned ways to overcome it over the years."

"That has nothing to do with being stupid. My daughter's doctor told me she may have some learning abilities when she gets ahead in school. She's homeschooled, so right now, it's kind of hard to tell. But I have noticed her having problems with letters."

"Well, I can help you figure it out. I've been through enough tutors all my life."

"I would really appreciate that."

"You and your brothers don't seem like the Mafia type. I've always heard how ruthless you all are. Like my father."

"Make no mistake, Bella. I'm a stone-cold killer. But my brothers and my cousins and I are doing away with the old ways of our parents. There are better ways to rule, and that is to lead and protect. My father and uncle were ruthless and soulless. My mother still that way."

"Your mother is still alive? And she was cruel to you and your brothers?"

"Yes, she is still alive. She's visiting her sister in Italy. She should be back in a few days. Her and my father were a perfect match. They were both ruthless and cruel to us boys. My father died, and she now knows her boundaries. She lives here but at arm's length. She is our mother, and with that, we have not cast her out. I've also figured out you're not a whore. You're way too innocent." She looks relieved at my words. "Can I ask how many men you've been with, if you don't mind me asking?"

With that question, she looked extremely nervous. She started shaking and dropped her head and stared at her hands on her lap. She whispered, "One."

"I knew your father was a liar. Is that the guy you lost your virginity to when you were fourteen?"

"Is that what my father told you?"

"Yes."

She started shaking, and now I was sorry I asked the question. I walked around, picked her up, and sat her in my lap.

"It's okay. You don't have to tell me. I was just curious because I know your father is a liar. I don't care how many men you were with, what, and when you lost your virginity. I just want you to be mine."

She released a long breath and weight that had been hanging over her for years.

"My virginity was stolen from me when I was ten," she said. She quietly let tears fall down her cheek and onto my shirt.

"What? Someone molested you? Who was it? If he is not dead, I will make sure he is soon!" I said through gritted teeth.

"My father," she said quietly.

"Fuck!" I said way too loud, and she flinched.

"It's okay, Bella. I'm not mad at you. I'm mad at that sick fucker for what he did to you. I know the physical abuse is fresh. How long did he rape you for?"

"The last time was a little over a week ago. His anger is the worst I have seen. Someone took down several of his locations, and he was angry. I hid because I knew it was coming. He was going to kill Vera if I didn't come out of hiding. I did what I was told."

She told me the horrific acts he did to her, and my heart just kept breaking for her. How could a father be so cruel to such a precious woman? And it just made me want her even more.

"Bella, I'm so sorry. This is my fault. I am the one who took down all his operations."

"It's not your fault. He has been hurting me for years."

"I can't take it back for you, Bella, but it will never happen again. I'll make sure he suffers before I end his pathetic life."

"Thank you for being kind to me."

"That's all I'll ever be to you.

"We need to have your stitches removed. I saw several on your back and butt. Do you want the doctor to do it?" She started breathing erratically. "Easy, Bella. Just talk to me, and we can figure this out."

"I have stitches everywhere." I looked at her, understanding what she meant.

"Your father tore you?" I asked through gritted teeth.

"In both places."

I closed my eyes and tried to breathe. This poor woman. "Oh, sweet Bella, what hell have you lived? What is going to make you comfortable?"

"I'm humiliated. I don't want anyone else to know."

"I'm going to be your husband. I know you don't know me yet, but my brothers and I have been through things too. I get humiliation. I'll remove them if you will let me. I've removed several in my lifetime." She nodded. "How would you like to do this? You want me start on your back first?"

"Yes."

"Okay, go get your pj's on and I'll meet you in your room." I got some scissors and tweezers and met her in her room. She was wearing red pj's.

"You look beautiful in pj's." She laughed. "Lay on your stomach and pull your top up." She did as I asked. He beat the hell out of her. I started removing them, and she lay still. I kissed her back occasionally.

"Okay, do you have any on your butt or legs?" She nodded. "Okay, I'll remove them. Pull them down, please." She stood up, and I grabbed a blanket and pulled it up behind her.

"You're covered, Bella." She removed them and lay back on the bed.

I pulled the blanket down in sections and covered her up as I went. I went all the way down the top of her thighs, and I didn't see any more.

"Now the hard part, Bella. Turn on your stomach and I'll cover you." She did as I asked. She looked petrified. "I'm sorry. I don't know any other way than just to do it. I will always take care of you." She nodded. "Spread your legs and I'll check them and remove them if they are ready."

She spread her legs wide, and she had tears in her eyes and looked away from me. I pulled the blanket up, and she had several stitches. I removed them out of her pussy first then the several around her ass. I was so pissed. I was going to do this and worse to him. I covered her up.

"All done," I said as I picked her up and carried her to the couch. We sat in front of the fireplace. I looked in her eyes.

"Bella, you want me to show you mine? It's not as pretty as yours." She burst out laughing. I was talking about my asshole, trying to distract her.

"I'll take a rain check." She made me laugh.

"Are you ready for bed? I'm sure you will sleep great after that meal."

She smiled at me, and I helped her out of my lap. "It's going to be a busy day tomorrow." I tucked her in. "Are you good?"

"Yes," she said. "Thank you for a great day. The best of my life."

"Oh, Bella, you're going to have a whole life of amazing days. I promise. I will be down the hall if you need me for anything."

I said good night and shut the door and headed to my bedroom. I was going to have to speak to my brother about what this poor girl had been through. Things might not have played out according to plan. But I was happy I was able to save her. I thought she would make a wonderful wife and mother.

I finally fell asleep around 1:00 a.m. I was awoken to cries of pain. I jumped out of bed, grabbed my gun, and headed down the hall toward the noise. It was coming from Annika's room. Vera was coming out of her room.

"She is having another nightmare, sir. I'll help her," Vera said.

"It's okay, Vera. I'll take care of her," I said.

Vera headed back to her room with a smile on her face.

I opened the door and closed it behind me. She was thrashing around.

"Please don't," she said in her sleep.

Her fucker of a father is going to pay! I climbed into the left side of the bed and started talking to her.

"Bella, it's okay, sweetie. You're safe here." I put my hand across her stomach. "I've got you. I won't let anyone hurt you." I lay beside her and pull her to me, her back into my chest. I wrapped my arm around her and kept whispering to her, "Your pain is over. He will never touch you again."

She settled down and snuggled into me more, and her breathing evened out. God, this felt so good. It felt perfect, like she was supposed to be here. God, what was she doing to me? She had only been here twenty-four hours.

I fell asleep with her next to me and slept the best night I ever had. She was beautiful laying there with the light starting to come through the windows. She was the light of my dark world. She started waking up and trying to stretch, but she was still against my chest. With my arm wrapped around her, she froze, and I knew what she was thinking.

"Bella, it's okay. You just had a nightmare, and I came to help you." She relaxed.

"I'm sorry I woke you up. I'll try not to do it again."

"Nonsense. You're going to be my wife. I'll protect you, even from nightmares. I've slept better next to you than I have my entire life." I was telling her the truth.

"Thank you for being here. It means so much," she said with tears in her eyes.

I kissed her on the back of her head. "You always smell so good, like light and fresh air."

She smiled at me.

"We have a long day today. Meeting the amazing Grazia, shopping for all the things you want for your room, and your wedding dress," I said.

"I'm looking forward to it."

"This is your room now. You want to stay in here or move to my room after we are married tomorrow?" She tensed up. "I'm not talking about sex. Don't get me wrong. I want to have sex with you, but if you never want to, I understand that. I would just be happy with you next to me." She relaxed.

"I'm sorry I'm so messed up. I wonder who I would be if this never happened to me. Would I be strong and confident?" she said.

"Bella, you are the strongest person I know. I adore you now, and I'll adore you when you start to spread your wings. We have a lifetime together. Don't ever be sorry."

"You're so good to me, and I don't understand it. I've never done anything for you to be kind to me, but I will never take advantage of it, Angelino."

"I know you won't. I feel it in my soul. Now let's get up and take a shower and get ready. I'll swing by and pick you up on the way down to breakfast. I have Maria getting with Vera today to show her where everything is so she can get started," I said to her. Both of us had to get our showers and get ready for the day.

Annika

Angelino came into my room to calm me, and he slept next to me all night. What kind of Mafia guy did that? He wanted me in his room after we were married. I wanted that. I didn't have another nightmare the rest of the night.

I was just not sure I could make him happy. I might never want sex. All I had ever known was violence.

I dried off and picked out a long flowing pink dress with flats since we were going to walk around. I put on some mascara and lip gloss and blow-dried my hair straight. I put it into a bun with ringlets around the bun and a couple of loose strands around my face. I spritz on a little perfume and then went out the door. Angelino was standing outside my door, waiting for me in his suit of choice.

"Shall we?" he said as he reached for my hand.

"I'm going to have to use the GPS on my phone for this mansion," I said. We both started laughing.

"It will take some time, but you will be running this house before you know it. You'll know where everything is."

"I will be running this house?"

"Yes, Annika. This house will be yours as much as it is Giovanni's and mine. You are going to be my wife and the wife of a don. You will be my partner. You can decorate and hire and fire staff as you wish. You can plan the menus. I would leave Giovanni's wing and Antonio's wing alone. Everything else, you can change as you wish."

"Who is over it now?" I asked as we continued to walk toward the dining room.

"My mother."

"Is she going to be upset?"

"Absolutely. She loves power and control, and this is the last she will have. Don't worry. She will deal with it or leave. I want your hand and spirit around the mansion. This thing has been in the past for way too long."

"I think I would love to redecorate, if you are okay with that." He smiled down at me.

"Have I told you how stunning you look this morning?"

I blushed and look away. "Thank you, Angelino. You make me feel beautiful."

As we entered the dining room, I noticed it was huge and had the biggest rectangular table I had ever seen. It held thirty-two people. There were large double French doors in the back where the terrace was, where we had dinner in last night. There was a huge fireplace against the left wall and buffets against the right wall for serving. The head chair was closest to the terrace doors. On the right side was Grazia, I presumed, and his brother was beside her. On the left was another grumpy-looking man.

"Good morning, everyone," Angelino said.

Giovanni stood up and grabbed my free hand with both his hands. "Good morning, Annika. We are happy you can join us," Giovanni said to me.

"Hey, sweetie. I want you to meet someone. This is Annika."

"Hi," she said with a huge smile.

"Hello. You're such a beautiful little girl," I said to her.

"I'm not little. I'm five, and Daddy says I'm a big girl," she said, and I laughed out loud.

"Yes, I guess you are, but you are still beautiful."

"Thank you," she said. "You're very pretty too," she told me as her father smiled at me.

He walked over to her and puts her in her seat. He grabbed my hand and led me around the table.

"Salvatore, this is my soon-to-be wife, Annika," Angelino said to the man who was still sitting. He stared at the us both.

"To your feet now! Respect your superior or else I will remove you!" Angelino bellowed at Salvatore. The man stood up and nodded to me.

"Annika," he said.

"It's nice to meet you, Salvatore," I said.

"Move down a seat. This chair now belongs to Annika."

"I'm no longer hungry," Salvatore said, walking out of the room.

"He used to be second-in-command under my father. I made Giovanni second-in-command. He is all about the old ways and does not change," Angelino told me as he moved the chair out for me to sit in. He put a new plate in front of me.

"I loved the look on his face," Giovanni said, laughing.

"Grazia, honey, I wanted to tell you something. Annika and I are getting married. She is going to be my wife tomorrow," he said to his daughter.

"Daddy, does that mean I will have a mommy now?" she asked her father. Angelino looked at me for guidance.

"I would love that," I told her with a smile. Angelino let out a slow breath.

"Oh, I would. Can I call you Mommy?" she asked.

"I would love that, if your father doesn't mind," I told her.

"If that's what you want, Grazia, I'm good with you calling her Mommy." Her big smile matched Giovanni's next to her. He was happy for Grazia.

"So you are getting married tomorrow?" Giovanni asked.

"Yes. We want it soon for her protection and before Satan gets back here," Angelino said to his brother. He was talking about his mother.

"What do you need me to do to help?" Giovanni asked us both.

"We want a simple beach wedding. Just us with our cousins. We are going to pick a dress for her and Grazia. Get our tuxes ready and have Maria set the ceremony up," Angelino said.

"I can do that. I want Amelia to come, but she is worried about the bruising still. And she is so shy and scared around everybody," Giovanni said.

"I can speak to her if you like. I still have bruises everywhere, and my black eye is still noticeable. We can pick her dress and shoes if she does not want to go out," I said to Giovanni. Giovanni looked at Angelino.

"Oh god, did I say something wrong? Did I step over the line? I shouldn't have spoken. I'm sorry," I said and put my fork down and looked at my hands in my lap. Angelino put his hand over mine and squeezed.

"You can always say what is on your mind. You are allowed to speak and have your own mind. We're just happy at your genuine selflessness. Wanting to help someone else when you're suffering yourself. I made the perfect choice to marry you. You'll be a queen in this organization," Angelino said to me. I looked in his eyes, and I could tell he was being truthful. Giovanni was smiling at me.

"I would love for you to speak with her," Giovanni said.

"I'll see her after breakfast."

We continued to eat as Giovanni and Angelino talked business. I looked around, and my eyes kept going to the terrace. I would have the door open and plants all over the terrace with twinkling lights at night. I would love to see the garden. I wondered how beautiful it was. This room was so dark and heavy. I guessed that was a Mafia thing.

"What are you thinking about?" Angelino asked me.

"This place is amazing. It's just dark," I said.

"I agree. This was our father's look. We have always wanted to make changes. We just have not. What are you thinking?"

"It's a beautiful day. I would have all the doors open or at least all the blinds pulled back. That way, you can feel the wind from the lake. I would add some lighter furniture to the dark and replace all the artwork. It's very dark with all the battles."

"I love it already. Get everything of our father's and mother out of here," Giovanni said.

"I love the table, but if it was in a light gray, it would help. I'd add some plants to the terrace."

"These are great ideas. Let me get with a contractor of ours, and we will make all the changes you like," Angelino said.

"Where are your gardens located? I would love to see if there is seating and such. It would be a good place to read."

"We don't have any gardens. Our mother always said it wasn't necessary and a waste of time. I'll get with the groundskeeper, and you can tell him what you want."

"Thank you for allowing me to add some life to this place." Angelino only smiled.

"I'm going take Grazia to Maria to get her lesson started. I'll see you in a few when you speak with Amelia," Giovanni said to me.

They left the room, so it was just Angelino and me.

"You never answered me if you wanted to stay in your room or move to mine."

"I would love to be with you."

"Wonderful. We'll go look at my room and make a new list of what you want changed. We start there today."

"Let's go look at it," I said, way too excited. I never had freedom or a choice about anything. This was very new to me, but it felt like it had always been this way with him.

We headed up to his room. It was at the end of the hall. We entered, and the wall to the left was nothing but floor-to-ceiling windows, only the drapes were closed, and you couldn't see outside. It was really dark. I went over and pulled them all open. Wow, it was the same view as my room, but they were not windows, just doors that slid open to the balcony that looked over Lake Michigan. I left the doors open and came back in the room. His bed was a king-size bed opposite the door. There was a large carved headboard with animals on it. It was not very flattering. It was flanked by two night-stands. The walls were covered in a dark ugly wallpaper from like three decades ago. There was a large double fireplace about twenty-five feet from the bed to the right of it. There was only a large desk against the same wall as the bed.

"Do you work in here?"

"No, this was my parents' room. It gets passed down to the don. It was my brother's, and now it is mine. I hate this room. I only sleep here."

We walked into this stone bathroom. It had a huge walk-in shower with ten showerheads and a huge double tub. It was the same as my room but larger, and it had a shower. We continued to walk into the closet. It was an easy thirty by thirty feet with his things on one side.

"Your room is amazing."

"Thank you. I want you to do anything you want to it. Make this our sanctuary, a place of rest. Money is not an option."

"I have some great ideas—a seating area in your room and a reading nook and maybe a chandelier in the closet and more seating. Remove all the dark wallpaper and artwork."

"I'm on board with all of it. We will pick up some furniture today. Let's head down and speak to Amelia and go do our shopping."

We headed down to Giovanni's wing of the castle. It had the same dark decor. It was smothering. Giovanni let us in.

"Amelia, this is Annika, Angelino's soon-to-be wife," he introduced us.

"Hello," she said in a quiet voice.

"It's nice to meet you, Amelia," I said. Giovanni and Angelino walked out to the balcony.

"I'm getting married tomorrow, and I would love for you to be there standing next to me. I don't have anyone here I know."

"I don't know. My face is still all bruised up, and I don't look very pretty. I'm extremely thin, and I'm just not good with people," she said to me.

I turned my cheeks so she could see my bruised face. "Amelia, my father did this to me, and worse, I'm scarred all over. But Angelino makes sure I know I'm beautiful no matter what. The bruising will fade away in time. But the memories we make will last a lifetime. I would love for you to be part of those memories, and I know Giovanni would love you to be there. Will you please come tomorrow?" I asked her.

"Yes, I would love to. I must figure out something to wear," she said.

"I can pick something up today when I go out to get my dress and Grazia's dress. What size do you wear?" I asked. She looked at me.

"I sew. I would really love to make my dress and Grazia's, if you're okay with that. You can choose any color you like. I can show you the material if that's good with you?" she asked.

"Oh, I would absolutely love that. I wish we had more time. I would have you make my wedding dress too. Let's go look at the material, and I'll pick something out."

We headed to her sewing room and looked through all the fabric. I picked out a beautiful lavender color that would go beautifully with her skin tone and hair.

"Thank you for coming and also making the dresses. You're amazing," I told her. I said goodbye to them both, and we left.

"You're a miracle worker. Giovanni is going to be singing your praises from now on," Angelino told me as we walked out the door. I laughed at that statement.

We headed into town and went to some dress shops. I picked out a simple white dress for me and some floral headbands for all three of us to wear and flats since we were going to be on the sand. I did not let Angelino see the dress.

"Did you get everything you want?" Angelino asked me.

"Yes, I did. Thank you," I said to him with a large smile.

"Let's head to a couple more clothing stores and get some more clothes for you and Amelia. I'm sure she is tired of sweatpants and the clothes my brother picked out," he said and made me laugh.

"You know she does, so she has a couple outfits made." We both laughed.

"Yes, but let's buy her a few things while we're here. I think she would appreciate it."

He made me pick out about forty different outfits for myself and shoes and some for Amelia, along with more bras and panties. He had all the packages delivered to the house while we went to a high-end furniture store. As we walked in, this leggy redhead made her way over to us, ignoring me. She wrapped her arms around Angelino. He stiffened and did not let go of my hand.

"Angelino, I'm so glad to see you. It's been too long. I've missed you," she gushed. He let go of my hand and grabbed her by both arms and moved her off and away from him. Then he grabbed my hand again.

"I didn't realize you were back," Angelino said to the woman.

"Yes. I've been back a couple weeks now. Well, my singing career didn't go so well," she said.

"Neither did your art, acting, and ballet career," Angelino said to the woman.

She giggled and said, "Well, you know I'm a woman of many talents." She ran a finger down his chest in a seductive way. He grabbed her wrist and shoved her back slightly.

"Keep your hands to yourself, Sarah. Don't ever disrespect my wife again, or you'll pay with your life. Understood?"

He glared at her. She looked at him like she was going to pass out.

"Good. Now that we are clear, apologize to my wife," he said.

"I'm sorry, miss. I was out of line," she said.

"Yes, you were," I said. Angelino started laughing.

"Where's your father?" he asked the woman.

"I'll go get him," she said.

"You're not jealous, are you, Bella?" he asked me.

I blushed. "I didn't like her touching you," I told him as I stared in his eyes. And I didn't. I saw red, and I was also hurt he was being touched by someone else. Then he set her straight.

"The feeling is mutual," he said, leaning in and kissing my cheek.

"I'm sorry about that. She is a gold digger who has been after me for years. Her father is a friend of the family."

"It's fine. Thank you for handling it."

"No one will ever come between us. We are a team."

We walked around, and the girl's father took down lists as I picked out furniture. I got a large black couch, two large wingback chairs in a light blue color, a large white area rug, and a chaise lounge for the closet. We ordered some outdoor furniture for the terrace and a double lounge love seat and an end table for the reading nook.

"I think we have a good start on the bedroom," I told him.

"Yes, we do. It's going to be great. I know you hate my bed. What do you want to do about that?"

"I love the canopy bed in my room. It would be amazing with some sheer material added to it. But I didn't want to make your space about me."

"I hate the bed. But we can swap them out."

"I think it will look great," I said and kissed him on his cheek. He looked at me, surprised. He smiled at me.

"We will have the contractor out after our wedding and remove the wallpaper and paint and add the chandelier that you picked out."

"I can't wait to see how it turns out, and we can add some of the finishing touches as we grow our life together," I told him.

"Can we get someone to take pictures of our wedding?"

"Of course. I'll text Giovanni and make sure he finds a photographer for tomorrow."

"Thank you very much for everything."

"You never have to thank me. Taking care of you and spoiling you is a privilege." We made it back to the mansion, and he took me to the dining room, where the table was set for two. Everyone else, I'm sure, had eaten already.

"I had the chef make our lunch. Lobster with some steamed veggies. I guess I should have asked if you liked seafood."

"I like it, but I'm highly allergic to it," I told him. He had a look of horror on his face like he was going to kill me with my lunch.

"I'm just kidding," I told him with a belly laugh. He looked at me and started laughing too. God, I didn't ever remember laughing. He made me comfortable. I had a sense of humor. Who knew?

"You had me on that one," he said.

We enjoyed our lunch and waited for the deliveries to come so I could organize everything.

Angelino

"Hey, brother, where's your amazing fiancée at?" Giovanni asked me as he entered our office.

"She is redecorating our room and putting away all her new clothes."

"I really appreciate all the clothes. Annika did a great job picking them out for Amelia."

I smiled at him. "I spoke to Amelia's father this morning to let him know we had his daughter and she was safe. He wants her back as soon as possible. I explained to him it may be a couple weeks because we are in the middle of taking down Volkov. I told him he could come here, and I gave Amelia a phone so they could FaceTime. He seems good with that for now."

"When we meet with her father, I will tell him my intent to marry his daughter."

"I'm happy for you, brother. Do you love her?"

"I know it seems fast, but I do love her, and I feel a strong connection with her. Now I just need to convince her father without starting another war."

"I'll go with you to Philadelphia, and we can show a united front. I'll leave Annika here to continue decorating and settling."

"I would appreciate the support."

"We will make sure we have people ready to come with us if things go south," I said.

"Maybe we should take a team with us and leave them on the plane."

"That's a great idea. Be prepared for the worst."

"It looks like Annika has turned into a blossoming flower since you brought her here. She seems to have fallen in love with you overnight," Giovanni said to me with a big smile on his face.

"She is not the only one. She sets my soul on fire. After the hell her father put her through, she deserves the world handed to her. And I'm going to make sure that happens."

"You know I'm worried about Satan returning. She is horrible, and it's going to get worse when she finds out you married a Russian the day before and did not tell her."

"Yeah, and you're engaged to a Greek. Oh, how the world turns," I said, and we both laughed.

"We must think of the fallout," Giovanni said.

"I'll make sure the guards keep an eye on Annika when I'm gone. If she does cause issues and not heed my warnings, then I will send her packing back to Italy with her sister with no support," I said.

"Then we agree. We need to watch Salvatore. Make sure there's no further issues," Giovanni said, looking over at me.

"I could have slit his throat for the way he spoke to her this morning," I told him.

"I'm headed back to my wing to be with Amelia. I'll see you tomorrow," Giovanni said as he walked out of my office.

I headed up to see my gorgeous fiancée. All the furniture was placed, and it looked amazing, bright, and warm. I walked through the closet, where she was sitting on the floor, sobbing. I dropped down and wrapped my arms around her.

"What's going on, Bella?" I asked her.

"He…he called me and has been texting. I didn't give him my number." She sobbed, talking about her father.

"Let me see your phone." She handed it to me, and I read the messages.

> You got rid of your phone and didn't give me your new number. Then you hang up on me when I call. Who the hell do you think you are? I told you before you left how this was going to

go. You better call me now and give me what I asked for.

This is not going end well for you if you betray me.

So your fucking ass thinks you can get married without telling me? You better tell that fiancé of yours we had a deal. He does not want to cross me. I'll end both of you.

"What did he say when he called?"

"He wanted me to tell him what I learned about you and your organization. He said I would be back with him before I know it and we would get our special time together. He is going to take me back. I'm scared, Angelino," she said, sobbing.

"Don't be afraid. You're safe here with me. I will not allow him to hurt you again, Bella. Your father is no match for us."

"How did he get my number?"

"I don't know, but I'll find out." I called Luca.

"Yes, boss," Luca said, answering the phone.

"I need you to divert all incoming calls and texts from numbers that are not programmed into Annika's phone. Make sure all the guards' and the drivers' numbers are programmed into her phone. I also need to find out who gave her number to her father," I said into the phone to Luca.

"I'll do it right now, boss," he said.

"Thank you. You're worth your weight in gold."

"Of course. I'll remember that come payday." We both laughed. I ended the call, focusing back on Annika.

I deleted the texts and her father's phone number.

"Here's your phone back, Bella. He won't bother you again." I kissed her on her head and pulled her into my lap.

"You should be an interior designer. You have such real talent. Our room is so warm," I said, trying to distract her from her situation. "It make me wants to stay in here locked up with you all day."

She laughed and said, "I really love decorating. It's fun. My father would never allow me to do things like this or have beautiful clothes like the these. It's like a dream."

"Well, you deserve it all. You never have to work, but if you get bored and like to open a business, you would be great at decorating." She laughed and went quiet for a second, like she was thinking about something.

"I'm actually a doctor," she said and left it at that.

"What? What do you mean?" I looked into her eyes.

"I'm Dr. Annika Volkov as of about three weeks ago. But I guess it will be Dr. Annika Rossi as of tomorrow."

"I'm confused. Your father allowed this?"

"Well, he allowed me to go to classes because he thought I was an idiot and he thought it would help me be smarter. He had no clue what I went to school for. I think he allowed me to go to school because of the hell he put me through to clear his conscience."

"Annika, that's amazing. We're going celebrate you graduating. After the wedding, we can throw a huge party. What do you think?"

"It would be great to celebrate it instead of hiding it."

"So what is your plan on becoming a doctor?" I asked her.

"I want to be a surgeon. I got accepted into Chicago's Memorial Hospital internship program, and it starts in about six months. But I have not contacted them back. My father wouldn't have allowed it."

"If you want to be a surgeon, then that's what you're going to be. Call and accept the internship. We will get you everything you need."

With tears in her eyes, she said, "You will allow me to work and finish my residency?"

"Of course, I would. You're brilliant, and you deserve this." She looked shocked and at peace all at once.

"Oh, thank you," she said as she wrapped her arms around me with excitement and put her head on my chest.

"You're so welcome, Bella. I want you in my bed tonight. I will be a gentleman. We can light the fireplace and bring our dinner up and eat at the new table." She got a table that sat two and put it in front of one of the balcony doors that was close to the fireplace.

Along with that, she got a seating area in front of the fireplace. It was very warm.

"I say yes to all of it," she said.

That's how we spent our night. We had our dinner in our room and talked about our lives and what our futures would look like. It was nice having something other than the Mafia to talk to.

I came out of the shower wrapped in the towel. She was in the closet. She stopped dead in her tracks, and her face turned beet red.

"I'm sorry. I didn't mean to make you uncomfortable."

"You're not, Angelino. You are just…just gorgeous," she said as her eyes dropped to the floor in embarrassment. I walked over to her, and she looked up at me.

"Thank you for saying that. May I kiss you?"

She nodded, and I put my lips to hers in a gentle kiss. But she parted hers, inviting me in. I put one hand on her hip and explored her mouth. My dick pressed into her stomach, but she did not back away. I pulled back and kissed her on the tip of her nose, not wanting to overwhelm her. She was breathless and had a dazed look in her eyes.

"Your lips do things to me," I said to her as I kissed her neck. She flushed even brighter.

I grabbed a pair of sweats because I didn't want to make her uncomfortable sleeping naked next to her. She was facing the other way, so I dropped my towel and put on my sweats. I looked up to see her naked backside before she got into the tub. Holy shit, she might be scarred, but she had a nice round ass. She was still way too thin but still gorgeous. I walked out of the closet and into the bathroom and looked over at her in the tub.

"You look relaxed." She was neck-deep in bubbles.

"It feels amazing. I only had a shower at my father's. Why are you looking at me like that?" she said, eyeing me staring at her.

"If I'm being honest, it's because I want to get in with you," I said. I could not tell what she was thinking.

"Oh, I…I…" she tried to speak.

"It's okay, Annika. You have been through a lot, but I was being honest with you. There is no pressure. Enjoy your bath," I said as

I leaned over and kissed the top of her head, getting a peek of her breasts as the soap cleared away from it.

I moved out of the bathroom into the bedroom. She had gorgeous breasts, not large but not small. She was perfect. I sat on the couch until she appeared in her satin pj's. *Fuck, it's going be a long damn night*, I thought to myself.

We got in bed, and I pulled her close to me, her back to my front. I kissed her good night. I slept so good with her by my side.

I woke up with her laying over my body, her leg over mine, her head and casted arm on my chest. *So this is what heaven feels like*, I thought to myself. I ran my hand along her back and kissed her head. She turned her head to look at me.

"Oh, good morning."

"Good morning, Bella. Are you ready to be Mrs. Rossi?"

"More than anything else."

"Me too. How about we go down for breakfast and put the finishing touches on today?"

She smiled at me, and she leaned up and kissed me softly and then slid out of the bed and into the bathroom. And there went my dick, just from her lips touching mine. This was going to be pure torture.

We headed down to breakfast where my brother, daughter, and Salvatore were sitting. Salvatore was still sitting in Annika's chair. Fucking great. This was going to be fun. I made my way around the table and greeted my brother and loved on my daughter for a minute. Salvatore just didn't make a move to leave Annika's seat.

"Salvatore, I'm pretty sure I told you yesterday this chair belongs to Annika," I said, glaring at him. Salvatore stood up.

"This seat belongs to me from your father, not to some Russian whore," he said.

And I fucking lost it. I hit him so hard he flew over the back of the chair and hit the floor. I punched him several times until my brother pulled me off him and the guards came running in. I stood up, seething.

"The only reason you sat at that this table in the fucking first place is because you were here when my father was alive. Now you have lost that privilege. But not before I remove your tongue from your mouth!" I yelled at him. "Take him to the basement. I'll deal with him tomorrow." The guards removed him, and I turned to Annika.

"I'm so sorry for that. You won't ever have to hear him again, Bella."

She just looked at me. I pulled her chair out for her, and she sat down. I put my hand on hers and pulled her chair to look at me.

"Are you okay? Have I scared you?"

"No, you protected me."

I looked in her eyes, and something was wrong. "Then what's going on?"

"How many others are going to hate me?" she asked with sadness in her voice.

"Whoever comes at you, I will remove from our lives. We are getting married today, and it's going to be the first day of the rest of an amazing life." I reached over and kissed her. "I'm sorry you and Grazia were here for that. Let's eat and enjoy our day. I can't wait to make you my wife."

"Don't be sorry. You did what needed to be done. And I can't wait to be your wife. And Grazia's mother."

We ate breakfast and both went to our rooms to get ready for the ceremony.

"I've never wanted anyone so much," I said to her at her bedroom door. "I have a hair stylist and makeup artist coming to help you ladies get ready for the day. I figured it might make Amelia feel better if her bruises were better covered. The artist is bringing a lot of extra makeup and products if you ladies want to keep any."

"You're so thoughtful. Thank you. I'm going to get ready now."

I pulled her in for a long kiss. "I can't wait to be your husband. I'll see you in a couple hours, Bella." She kissed me back.

She headed upstairs to get ready. The makeup artist showed up and spoiled her and Amelia, and they kept a bunch of makeup and hair styling products.

As time got near for the ceremony, they headed downstairs. The guards escorted them to the beach. Amelia walked down the aisle with Giovanni. As soon as Annika stepped on the beach, my heart stopped. She was wearing a white knee-length dress and had a ring of flowers around her head that matched Amelia's and my daughter's. She was stunning. I had never wanted any one so much in my entire life. She walked down the aisle by herself, and when she made it to the front, I took her hand and kissed her cheek.

"You look gorgeous."

"You're the sexy one," she said as she eyed me up and down.

The pastor started the ceremony, and we both repeated after him. We exchanged rings. I slipped her ring on her finger that I purchased. I got the engagement ring in a teardrop shape and five carats because she deserved it.

"I pronounce you man and wife. You may kiss the bride," the preacher said.

I reached over and put my hand on her face. I leaned in and put my lips to hers. We exchanged a passionate kiss that almost put me on my knees. My family was hollering and congratulating us as we headed toward the house. We were having a small reception with our family and a lot of food. The reception was on the terrace with a bunch of beautiful plants and flowers all around. She had fairy lights hung on all the shrubs and above the arch. The entire place looked magical. I thought to myself how she belonged here.

"This is where you're always meant to be. You look stunning, Mrs. Rossi."

"The Rossi name never sounded so good," she said, chuckling at me.

We cut our cake, and I made sure I got it on her face. She was laughing so hard, and I knew in that moment that she was going to get through this and come out on top.

"Come here, Grazia," Annika said to my daughter. She ran over to Annika. "Do you want to help cut the cake?" Annika asked her.

"Yes," she said, jumping up and down. Annika picked her up and put her on her hip, and she handed me another piece of cake and one to Grazia.

"Give your dad a bite of your cake, and he will give you a bite of his," she said. She did what she said. The photographer snapped pictures the entire time. Annika kissed her cheek and put her down, and she ran to her uncle.

The chef made a buffet-style layout across the tables. We wanted casual. We took a ton of pictures with everyone and then sat at a small table with Giovanni and Amelia. Annika was looking around in thought.

"What are you thinking about?"

"We should put a playground out here among the future garden for Grazia and all the other babies."

"You want my babies?" I said, chuckling.

She blushed. "I meant for Giovanni's future children and ours and any of the servants who have children. But to answer your question, I want to be Grazia's mother, and I want lots of babies with you," she said, smiling at me.

I pictured her swollen belly with my child, and that did several things to me.

"Then we will work on that immediately," I said, joking.

"Down, tiger," she said. "We have time." She smiled.

"When you're ready." I kissed her lips again.

"I love this woman of yours. She is so going to piss Mother off with the gardens and the playground and all the changes," Giovanni said.

"Yes, it will piss her off. This fits into the changes we are making. It's time to take things into the next generation," I said to the table. I raised my glass for a toast.

"To the new generation and to change," I said.

Everyone clanked their glasses together. A slow song came on.

"May I have this dance?" I asked Annika.

"Yes, you may," she said. She put her hand in mine. She put her arms around my neck, and my arms went around her waist. I put my chin on top of her head.

"I want to thank you for saving me, Angel. I would never have had a life if you did not get me away from my father. But also, for how you treat me. I will never take you for granted."

"Bella, it's only been a few days, but…" I hesitated for a second. "I'm in love with you."

She looked up at me with those big tear-filled eyes.

"I'm in love with you too."

We kissed a long and tender kiss. Another slow song came on, and I looked over to see my daughter staring at us.

"You want to dance with us?" I asked my daughter. She ran and jumped in my arms. Annika laughed, and we wrapped our arms around each other and danced. The only person missing in our family was my older brother. He would be so happy for us now.

Clink, clink, clink. Giovanni hit a spoon against his glass.

"We are the Rossis. We are fierce and loyal, and now it looks like we're lovable." All the Rossis bust out laughing, staring at me all hugged up with my family. "Love is not a weakness. Love is a fuel. The type of fuel that will burn cities to the ground to protect. Annika, we are even stronger with you joining our family. Welcome," he said.

Everyone erupted into cheers.

It was almost midnight, and Grazia was asleep on my shoulder. We thanked everyone, took Grazia to my room, put her in her pj's, and tucked her in.

I picked Annika up as we went to our room, and she squealed.

"I'm carrying you over the threshold for our wedding," I said to her as she laughed. I set her down on her feet and closed the door behind us. She had not moved from the spot.

"I'm going to hold you and love you like I do every night and nothing more right now," I said to her as I hugged her.

"I don't want to disappoint you. I'm just so broken."

"Bella, you could never disappoint me. You are so beautiful, smart, and kind. And we will work daily on putting the broken pieces back together."

"Thank you, Angel." It was her new favorite nickname for me.

"Always," I said as I smacked her ass. "Let's get ready for bed."

I went to the closet and stripped out of my tux and got ready to put some sweats on. As I looked up, I could see Annika in the bathroom, staring. I turned around to give her the full view. She didn't say anything. She just looked at me. I stepped up to her, fully naked.

CYNTHIA SEIDEL

"Bella, is there something on your mind? I'm your husband. You can tell me anything."

"I've never seen a man naked. I always closed my eyes. I have nothing to compare you to, but you remind me of a Greek god from my books," she said to me with a blush.

"That's the highest compliment I've ever gotten. If I'm the god, then you're the goddess. May I help you out of your dress?"

"Yes, please."

I walked around her. "Do you want me to leave so you have privacy?"

"No. You're my husband, and you'll have to see the extent of the damage at some point," she said, dropping her dress. She stood there with no bra and only white panties. She was facing the mirror so I could see all of her. She had scarring all over her back, ass, and legs, but it didn't take away from her beauty. She needed to put some weight on, but she was gorgeous. Her breasts were beautiful with tan nipples.

"Bella, your few scars only add to your beauty. You are fierce and look the part," I said to her, coming up behind her so I could be flush up against her. Her warmth radiated through my body as I pressed into her back. I rubbed my hand over her stomach and her neck.

"That feels so good," she said to me. I continued and rubbed my fingertips along her ribs and close to her breasts. She sucked in a breath.

"I want you to be comfortable. We're not having sex tonight. I want you to relax. If you want me to stop, then I will stop. This is all about you." She nodded in response. I continued kissing her neck and ears, and I rubbed a thumb across her nipple. She moaned, and it made my dick twitch. I continued rubbing my thumb on her nipples, and she was totally relaxed, enjoying the sensation. I moved to the other nipple and did the same. I moved my other hand along the top of her panties, and her body responded to me. I continued to talk to her, telling her how sexy she was and the things she did to me. I moved my hand down farther in her panties, and she had a small line of trimmed hair I could feel. I moved my palm over her clit.

104

"Oh god, that…that feels so good," she whispered. I picked her up and lay her on the bed. I kept reassuring her.

"This is about you only. No sex. All you must do is say stop." She nodded again. I lay down beside her, and I put my mouth on her right nipple and my hand on the other nipple. I licked and rubbed until she was moaning loudly and moving her hips up. I moved my hand underneath her panties while I continued to lick her nipple. I rubbed her clit softly and slowly and slid my finger to her slit.

"Oh, please," she said. I took that as an invitation and put my middle finger inside her. "Oh god," she whispered.

I kissed my way down her stomach and pulled her panties off. She looked down at me but said nothing. I put my mouth on her clit and slid two fingers inside her little body. She raised her hips, wanting more. I rubbed my tongue over her clit softly.

"God, you taste and smell so good."

I could ram a hole through the brick wall with the hard-on I had. I worked my fingers in and out of her a little faster while licking her clit.

"Angelino…oh, Angelino…oh god…oh god!" she screamed as she reached her orgasm, spasming around my fingers.

I was in heaven. I kissed my way back up her body and kissed her lips. She opened her mouth to let me in.

"I love you, Bella."

"I love you too," she said.

I moved off her enough to pull the blankets over her and shut the lamp off. I got under the covers with her and pulled her to me. My erection hit her backside.

"What about you?" she said.

"It's about you, Bella. I wanted to take care of you. I'll be fine."

"Angelino, I've never had…" She trailed off.

"I know. It's okay. I am going to be your first for lots of things."

She fell asleep fast, but it took me a little bit longer with this hard-on of the century.

I woke up as light peaked through the windows. She was laid on her back. I put my mouth over her beautiful breast, and she moaned. She started lifting her bottom up and moaning loudly. I glided my hand between her lips and felt that she was really wet. I circled her clit slowly.

"Oh, oh," she whispered. I started moving faster. "Angel, I'm going to…" She moaned loudly as she came hard, her body racked with tremors. I moved up and kissed her lips.

"Good morning, wife."

She opened her eyes and wrapped her arms around me.

"Good morning," she said with a smile. "Let's get showered and head down to breakfast. My mother will be here in a few days, and I want to prepare you for her behavior."

Annika

After Angelino made me come twice and took nothing in return, we headed down to breakfast. We were the first ones there. I walked over and opened all four terrace doors to allow the sun and wind inside.

"What a beautiful morning," I said.

"It's beautiful because you're in it," Angelino said, coming up behind me and wrapping his arms around me. I leaned into him and joined the heat and comfort.

"I love you, Angel. You have given me a beautiful life."

"I love you, Bella, and you deserve nothing but the best."

"I'm meeting with the contractors today on painting and for the chandelier in the room. The landscape designer will be here today also. You're okay with me handling all of this? No matter what I want?"

"Absolutely. The place has been in the last century way too long. It's dark and gloomy. I love all the ideas and the playground."

"I'm going to change the dining room around also, and when these are complete, I will move on to another room."

"I can't wait to see what you come up with. My mother is going to hate everything you do. She is a wicked woman. You are now the head of the house and my queen. In our family, women can hold power. That means we are partners. You'll have a say in knowledge of whatever is happening all the time, if you choose to.

"My mother was pissed when my father died and she did not keep her throne. When you have boy heirs, they step into their father's place.

"I never knew the Italians run the family like that. In the Russian Mafia, we were not even allowed to speak. Women are a bargaining tool."

"Many families are run the same way. When my brother became don, he did not want one person having that much power. He had the final decision, but we all had equal say. We came up with a plan to turn things around. Our people feared us and hated us. My father used them and extorted money from already struggling families. We put an end to all that, along with the skin trade."

"That is inspiring, a united front with your people who now support you and will be loyal. That's a brilliant idea," I said to him. He smiled at me.

"Bella, you are the brilliant one. You can see what I'm doing and have only been here for a few days, and my mother and Salvatore refuse to see it. They say we will look weak and be vulnerable."

I laughed. "Oh, I'll tell you this. My father fears the Rossis. He knows your power, and that's why he allied himself with you."

"God, you're so intelligent, Bella."

That made me smile even brighter, and that smile of his added something to the heat. *He thinks I'm intelligent and not stupid.*

"Thank you. That really means a lot to me."

He kissed my forehead. "I know you're new to all this. But the Rossi men are here to protect you and to help you. I need you to tell me when something is said or done by my mother when I'm not around. It needs to be handled fast so she knows she has no power."

"I will. I'm just afraid I may not be queen material," I said, feeling weak.

"You're the strongest person I know, Bella. You have walked through hell and have come out on top. What happened to you can't be undone, but it will make you who you are. You are not weak. You just don't know any better yet. You are not chained anymore. And you grow more every day. Don't be afraid of anything you want to do."

We took a seat and ate.

"Are you dealing with Salvatore today?" I asked him.

"Yes. After breakfast, Giovanni and I will head down." He looked at me as if he was trying to read me.

"What is your plan for him? Will he still have a seat as one of your men?"

"I really don't know what to do with him. He will not have a tongue at the end of the day. But if I send him away, I can't watch him. He might bring some of my men against me that were loyal to my father." He looked up at me, trying to read me. "What is it, Bella? You look like you have something you want to say, but you are afraid to say it."

I looked at him. He gave me the space to breathe and make my own way, so I told him what I was thinking. "Why not make him a guard? One on the outside of the house. You remove his tongue and remove him from his seat, and everyone will know you're not weak, but your punishment is just," I said to him. He looked up at me blankly.

"God, Bella, I have chosen the perfect woman to be queen. That's a perfect situation. And everyone will know the next step is death if he steps out of line."

I smiled at him and reached over. I kissed him and looked in his eyes. I saw so much love.

"My brother and I are going out of town for two days to Philadelphia. I need to meet with Amelia's father. I'm leaving the day after tomorrow. I'll make sure you're well protected."

"I understand. Grazia and I will be fine. We have decorating to do."

"I also need to speak with your father. The newspaper will have put our wedding on the front page. He is going be fuming. But our alliance is complete."

"I have not heard anything from him," I said.

"All his calls and messages are being diverted. I know what he says, but you won't get them," he said, looking up at me.

"What has he said?" I asked.

"Do you really want to know? I'll tell you, but I prefer to deal with him my way."

"Truth is, Angel, I don't want know. I will let you handle him." I didn't want to know. He had consumed enough of my life.

"Thank you for trusting me with this."

"I trust you with everything."

Just as I said that, Grazia ran in the dining room and jumped straight into my lap.

"Well, good morning to you too," I said to her.

Angelino laughed out loud at his daughter.

"Mommy, can you play outside with me today?" I looked at Angelino, and I saw tears in his eyes.

"Of course we can. What do you think about building a playground in the backyard?" I asked her.

"Oh, with the slide and the swing?" she said with enthusiasm.

"Yes, like that. You can help me design it. We will add whatever you want to it."

"Yes! Yes! Yes!" she said, full of energy.

The chef brought in her breakfast and looked at me, not sure where to put Grazia's plate.

"She'll be in my lap today," I said to him, and he smiled and set her plate down in front of me. She dug in and ate with gusto.

"I'm done. Can we go make the playground now?"

I laughed so hard I had tears in my eyes. "That's my cue," I said to Angelino. "Yes, let's go, baby girl," I said to her. I kissed Angelino on the head and headed out with Grazia for the day.

Angelino

God, what it does to my heart to see my daughter getting attached and her calling Annika Mommy.

"Are you ready to handle the prick in the basement?" I asked Giovanni as he entered the dining room.

"I'm more than ready."

We headed down to the basement, and Salvatore was chained to the ceiling. All four limbs were chained. He couldn't move. He looked up as I opened his cell door.

"I'm sorry. It won't happen again," he said very quickly.

"You're right. It won't. I let you keep a seat at our table for way too long. You served my father for years. That's the only reason I let you stay. You're stuck in the old ways and refused to look forward. You disrespected my wife, and my father would have had your head for that crime."

He did not reply to the statement because he knew it was the truth.

"What are you going to do with me?"

"You will no longer have a seat at the table. You will return as a guard on the grounds, but not before I remove your tongue."

"A guard? I belong at the table. I've earned it. You and your brother are weak, and you make the Rossi family weak," he said as my phone rang.

"Yes. Luca, what did you find?" I asked into the phone.

"Salvatore is the one who gave out Annika's number to her father and told him about the wedding," Luca said.

"Thank you. We are with him now," I said to Luca, hanging up. "You've been talking to Volkov?"

111

"He wanted her phone number, and I thought y'all had an alliance. I didn't know he was not supposed to have it." He looked at me like he was scared of what was going to happen.

"You have no say so anymore, so it does not matter what you think of my brother and me." I looked at Giovanni.

"Take two fingers for him calling us weak. Take another two for talking to Volkov without permission."

"No! No!" he screamed.

Giovanni cut off all four fingers on his left hand, and he screamed and pissed himself.

"Now who's weak?" Giovanni asked him, laughing.

"Open your mouth now. It's time for your tongue for disrespecting my wife."

He clamped his mouth shut. I laughed, and Giovanni hit him hard enough and knocked him out. We clamped his mouth open and put some smelling salts under his nose. He woke up with a start. He started shaking his head.

"Giovanni, get the cauterizer hot." I looked up at Salvatore's eyes.

"You step out of line a hair and next time, I will end your life!" I told him.

I reached in with some pliers and pulled his tongue out as far as I could. Giovanni steadied his head. I took the garden shears and cut his tongue out as far back as I could. He was making gurgling noises as he screamed with no tongue, and he passed out. I cauterized it, and he woke up thrashing again.

"Send the doc down and get him cleaned up," I said Giovanni.

"My pleasure," he said, laughing at Salvatore.

I left to head upstairs. I showered and changed and started to head back to my office. I saw Annika and Grazia outside in the yard. I laughed and watched Grazia explaining everything she wanted on the playground.

"My family," I said to myself.

I picked up the phone and called Volkov.

"About fucking time. I don't appreciate you ghosting me," he said.

I laughed. "I don't really care, Volkov. We're married. The alliance is sealed."

"I want my daughter to come stay a couple days. I miss her, and you won't let her talk to me," he said.

"Let's fucking get this straight right now, you sick fuck. Annika is mine. You will never see her again after the sick shit you did to her."

"She is a liar. She has mental issues, and we both know she's stupid. She's my daughter, and I have the right to see her."

"First of all, Annika is not fucking stupid. Shut your damn mouth about her. She's probably one of the most brilliant people I've ever met. Your daughter is a doctor, and you didn't even know it because you're the stupid fucker. And just to let you know a little tidbit of information. Annika's helping me run the Rossi family, and she's brilliant at it. When it's time to take your head, you can almost bet it's going to be your daughter giving the order."

She was flourishing here. All the things she wasn't allowed to do, she was allowed to do here. I just wanted her happy for her entire life.

"One day soon, she will be carrying my child. We will have the house full of our children. I know you molested her and beat her for years. She is happy here, and she never wants to see you or speak to you again. You'll pay for what you've done to her, one way or another."

"Fuck you, Rossi. We might have an alliance, but I'll see her again!" he bellowed and hung up.

"Wow, that went better than I thought," I said to myself with a laugh.

Giovanni

Angelino and I flew to Philadelphia to meet with Amelia's father. We had several men waiting in the jet in case they were needed. When we got to Amelia's house, she jumped out of the car when she saw her father by the door.

"Baba!" she hollered. I carried her up the stairs because her foot was still in a cast.

They embraced each other. Angelino and I stood back and watched.

"Thank you so much for bringing my daughter home to me safe," he said over his daughter's head.

"You're welcome, sir."

"I'm forever in your debt. Please come in so we can talk."

He did not even frisk us. He knew we were not a threat. We headed back to his big office. He had a couple of armchairs with a couch in front of the fireplace with a huge desk and a couple of chairs in front.

"Have a seat," he said as he pointed at the fireplace.

He poured us both some whiskey as he sat on the sofa with his daughter. We sat in the chairs. Her father knew what happened to her and that I had been taking care of her.

"He will pay for kidnapping you," her father said to her.

She just grabbed his hand, reassuring him. He looked up at me.

"I know you have an alliance with Volkov. Where does that put us when I kill him?" he said to me.

"What is said in this room stays in this room," Giovanni said to him. He nodded in agreement.

"Volkov killed our older brother and pinned it on you and a motorcycle gang. We've been planning on taking him down for months. We are the ones that burned all his properties to the ground. He wanted him to come to us for an alliance. The plan was for my brother to marry his daughter as a revenge tactic. But he has been abusing his own daughter for years. Our family is strong, and our plan is to take the rest of his assets, including his money. To kill him and all his top men and drive the Russians out of the city. We knew there was a war coming with you and him. But we did not know he had your daughter. We have the same goal as you," Giovanni said to him.

"What happens after he's dead?"

"We will own the city. We have no reason to come here and encroach on your territory."

"You saved my daughter and brought her safely home. I'll do whatever I can to help you take down Volkov. But what else can I do for you for saving my daughter?"

Giovanni took a deep breath, looked at the floor, and then looked at her father. "I want to marry your daughter, sir. Not for an alliance but because I want her as my wife."

Argyros stood up and started walking around the office like he was thinking. Amelia got up and went to her father. She grabbed his hand in hers and looked at her father.

"Baba, I know you have an arranged marriage set for me to secure another alliance, but I want to be with Giovanni, Baba. He and his family saved me and have been so good to me. I love him," she said to her father. He reached up and rubbed his thumb across her cheek.

"My beautiful, sweet daughter. I thought I would never see you again. I'm indebted to the Rossis for life for bringing you home safe." He released his daughter and walked over and stood behind the couch. "Giovanni, I know my daughter will be cared for. You have my blessing."

Giovanni stood up and shook his hand. "Thank you, sir. I will take good care of her. She can fly back anytime she wants."

Amelia wrapped her arms around her father. "Thank you, Baba."

"Of course, my child," he said to his daughter.

"Mr. Argyros, there's something else we need to discuss that might be quite sensitive and hard to hear," I said to her father.

"Go ahead and say what's on your mind."

I hold Amelia's hand because I know she was scared about telling her father. She still feared her stepmother was going kill them.

"Sir, your wife has been abusing Amelia for years."

He looked at his daughter just to see if it was the truth or not. "Amelia, is this true? Has Iris been hurting you?"

"Yes, Baba. I was scared to tell you. She threatened to kill you and my brothers." Amelia went into detail about all the abuse she endured over the years. Her father wrapped his arms around her and told her how much he loved her and how sorry he was.

"I will handle Iris. This I promise you."

"We also believe your wife has something to do with the kidnappings. Both of them. We have one of our tech guys looking into it. He is tracing phone calls to find out if she has any connections with Volkov. I just think you need to watch your back in the meantime until we figure it out."

"I'll secure her now. I'm not watching my back. I'll throw her in a cell," he said.

Angelino

We spent a few nights with Argyros and his family, meeting Amelia's five brothers. Their family was a lot like our own. By day 4, I was ready to get back to the Grazia and Annika. We flew back with Amelia. Her father was more settled now that he had seen his daughter. We pulled up to our mansion, and the first thing I noticed were potted flowers down the steps in a V formation.

"Wow, that looks great," Amelia said.

"Yes, it really does."

I stepped into the house, and light flooded in from every window. Annika opened all the drapes. That itself took the darkness out. It was early morning, so we made our way to the dining room, where they should be eating breakfast. I walked in, and Grazia and Annika were in their chairs, laughing about something. But what I noticed was the large dining room looked even bigger. The floors throughout the house were stone, giving the castle its charm. But the table was redone in a gray color, with vases of flowers in the middle. The buffet was now black and not brown. The bottom part of the wall was stone. We left it that way, but it was now whitewashed. Above the stone, the dark wallpaper had been removed and now painted a very light blue.

Annika blew up family pictures and put them above the fireplace. It was us dancing with Grazia. And there was a spot next to it, waiting for Giovanni's wedding pictures. She had a couple up-to-date pictures of Chicago landmarks put on the walls. The terrace doors were open. We could see the yard. It was covered in flowers and shrubs. She looked at us as we entered. Annika and Grazia jumped up to greet us.

"You're back," Annika said.

"Yes. I missed you. I could not get back fast enough," I said to her and Grazia.

"The place looks amazing," Giovanni said first.

"It really does, Annika. You outdid yourself," I said.

"Thank you. It was really fun."

"Wait until you see the playground. I did it," Grazia said.

"I can't wait to see it," I said.

"Let's go, Daddy. Let me show it to you," Grazia said with excitement.

She led me out the door of the terrace. The gardeners were still putting in flowers and trees. We already had several huge oaks and the three acres in front of at the beach. She had several large flowering trees. The playground was in front of the pool that was to the left. There were several oaks surrounding the playground. The playground was about a thousand square feet. It had everything a kid could want—merry-go-round, teeter-totter, rock climbing wall that led across a bridge to a playhouse, several tubes, slides, and monkey bars. It had benches so someone could sit and watch the children. The whole area had a ground perimeter around it that held in all the sand. Plants and things were added around it. It looked like it belonged there.

"You did an amazing job, Grazia. Do you like it?" I asked my daughter.

"I love it. Me and Anna have been playing on it," she said. Anna was one of the servant's daughters. They were the same age.

"I'm glad you love it." She ran to the playground, and Annika and I sat on the bench. Giovanni and Amelia headed to the house.

"I've missed you," she said.

"I really missed you," I said to her. I leaned in and kissed her slowly. She opened her mouth for me, and we both moaned at the same time. I pulled away, and I saw desire in her eyes.

"You're so beautiful," I said to her. She blushed as usual. "So what project is next?" I looked at her.

"Your office. It needs a woman's touch," she said. I looked at her like she lost her mind. She started laughing.

"I'm kidding." Seeing her at ease and happy did wonders to my heart.

"Thank God. I started to panic, picturing glitter walls and pink chairs," I teased her. We both laughed.

"I love you," she said.

"I love you more."

We worked into a routine. We had breakfast, and I worked on business stuff. She spent time with Grazia and redecorated this place. A month passed by fast, and my mother decided to stay a couple of weeks longer. She did not know I got married, or she would have been back already. It would be a blessing if she stayed gone.

Annika

My life had changed so much in the last couple of months. I was living and not just surviving. I loved Angelino and Grazia so much that it was hard to describe. I loved his family. I was getting more confidence every day as he allowed me to learn who I was. I accepted the residency, and we'd be doing that in about four months. I was so excited. Grazia and I had become close, and I loved being a mother. I couldn't wait to have a houseful of children and their cousins running around.

Angelino had not tried to have sex with me. He pleased me, and that was it. I had my cast removed last week, and I felt so alive. It was like I could breathe for the first time ever. Angelino and I had a date tonight at a high-end restaurant. It was at Angel's.

"What have you been up to today?" Angelino walked into the foyer of the house. I lifted my hands and did a 360 spin, showing him the foyer that I redecorated.

"What do you think? This is the first impression when you walk into our home. I want to feel alive, not dead," I said. We had double entry doors, and the foyer was huge with travertine flooring. There was a triple staircase that went to the left and right then to the back and then the same on the second and the main floor. Before the walls were all red velvet wallpaper from floor to ceiling and old family pictures of great-great-great-grandparents that started the Mafia. It was gloomy. Everything was so dark and brown and drab. Now all the wallpaper was removed and painted an off-white color with great entry tables with fresh flowers. I added art Grazia did to the walls, and I had all the pictures blown up. I removed the ugly red carpet and put down cream-colored rugs to lighten up this place.

"I love it. It finally looks like a home and not a morgue," Angelino said. "Are you ready to shower and get ready for a date?"

"Yes, I am." We walked to our room, and he headed to the shower.

I had been wanting him so bad, but I was nervous. As he went to shower, I decided to be bold. I had been here for almost two months. I needed him to know I was going to be good a good wife. I stripped in the room and headed to the bathroom. I was shaking, not used to being so bold. As I entered, he looked through the glass doors at me.

"Bella, what are you doing?" he said in a husky voice.

"I...wanted to shower with you. May I?" I dropped my head nervously.

"Absolutely. You can. You don't have to ask," he said, opening the shower door.

I stepped under the spray and wet my hair. I looked at him, and he was just standing there, staring at me.

"Have you washed yet?" I asked him to break the silence.

"Not yet," he said in a low voice.

I stepped out and grabbed his body wash and started to wash his shoulders. I worked my way down his arms and chest. He stood there, allowing me to explore him. His huge cock was at full attention since the moment I walked into the bathroom. I walked around and washed his back.

His ass looks like one of a god, I thought to myself. I washed the back of his legs and moved back around his front. I started with his feet and moved up to his legs until I got to his cock.

Don't lose it now. Be brave. Be brave, I kept telling myself. He was just watching me as I washed him. I reached for his cock, grabbed it, and washed it and his balls. He lost it.

"Oh my god, Bella, you're killing me," he said. I continued to stroke him more than a wash, and he opened his eyes and looked at me.

"I think we need to stop," he said as he put his hands over mine to stop me.

"Why? Have I done something wrong?" I asked, removing my hand. I felt deflated and not worthy. I dropped my head and backed away, feeling stupid. He did not answer me. I grabbed my shampoo and started washing my hair because I couldn't stand to look at him right now. I was afraid I might cry. I hurried and showered and got out before he did and headed to the bedroom. I had a robe on, and I was in the closet picking out a dress for tonight.

"Are you okay?" He came in the closet.

"Yes," I said as I continued to look through clothes.

"What's going on, Bella?"

I looked at him. "Nothing. I'm just getting ready."

He came up behind me and turned me to face him. "Why are you trembling?"

"I'm just cold, Angelino. I'll be good once I'm dressed. Thank you for taking me out," I said, trying to get him to stop asking questions.

He leaned forward to kiss me. I wanted him so badly, and he wouldn't even let me touch him. The kiss turned hungry, and I moaned. He opened my robe and found my clit, and he started rubbing. I was going to come if he kept going, but it would be one-sided again, and I didn't want that. I didn't understand why he didn't want me. I wanted to be desired, and I was not. I put my hands on his and used his words.

"We need to stop."

"What? What do you mean? Did I hurt you? I'm sorry. Did I go too far?"

I had my head down. "Not at all, Angelino. I just want the desire not to be one-sided anymore. I don't need relief. I'm good, but thank you," I said, stepping away from him. I walked around him and headed to our bedroom. I needed to step away from him.

"Bella, what's going on?" And then his phone rang.

"Yes? What? Fuck, I'll be there shortly," he said to the caller and hung up. "I have to go. I'm sorry about dinner. I'll make it up to you later," he said. He gave me a short kiss and left.

I guess there were worse things than not being desired. Like the hell I had been through. I would just keep my mouth shut and focus on whatever he wanted me here for, like being a mother to Grazia. Did he have a mistress? Or was it because I was so weak that he did not want to be with me? Why did my heart hurt so badly? I grabbed a book and headed to the sofa in front of the fireplace. I read for several hours with no word from Angelino. It was midnight already, and he was not here. Then I got a text.

> Angelino: I'm not going be home tonight. I'm staying at the penthouse.
> Me: Okay…do you want me to come there to be with you?
> Angelino: No need. I'll be home tomorrow. Good night.
> Me: Be safe. I love you, good night.

I did not get a response. What had I done wrong? Was I being too bold? Maybe I needed to calm down and keep my mouth shut. What had changed? I started crying before I knew it. I was up all night and couldn't sleep.

I walked down to the kitchen to get something to drink. I heard Giovanna talking to someone on the phone.

"You're not coming home tonight? Why? Annika is going to be upset. Who is the woman I hear? Is that Jessica? Brother, what the fuck are you doing?"

I got weak in the knees hearing him talk to Angelino about being with another woman. I backed up and hit a table behind me and knocked over a vase. It shattered on the floor. Giovanni looked up as I hit my knees.

"Annika, god, are you okay?"

I looked at him with tears running down my face. "I'm sorry." I got up, turned to run, and cut both my hands on the broken vase. I did not let that slow me down. I got to our room, and I slammed the door and slid down to the floor. God, I couldn't breathe. I was so stupid. So stupid. My father was right. Why? Why did he make me fall in love with him and then be with another woman? Was he really using me to get back at my father like he said? I ran to the bathroom and threw up. I was sobbing now. God, I was so pathetic. I needed out of here.

I called my driver because I knew they wouldn't let me walk out the gate. I didn't take anything but my purse and phone. My driver and two guards were waiting. I put a smile on my face.

"Where are we headed?" my driver asked.

I gave him the name of the restaurant that I knew I could lose my guards at. We entered the restaurant, and I ordered a drink and sat in the back. I ordered another one then headed to the bathroom. My guard followed me to the bathroom and waited outside the door. I went in and looked around. I opened the window and slipped through and dropped to the ground. I called a friend from school.

"Hey, Annika. It's been a while," James said.

"Yes, it has, James. I need your help," I said to him. I got to his house.

"Are you okay, Annika?"

"I will be, but I need your help, and fast. I have a GPS chip in my left butt cheek, and I need it removed before they find me."

He looked at me. "A GPS chip?"

"It's a GPS tracking chip. I need it out now, please, before they find me."

"I'm not sure I have everything I need here. I have no pain meds, just a scalpel and a few other things. What kind of trouble are you in?"

"Please, James. I can't talk about it," I said. He looked at me and could see the desperation in my eyes.

"I'll remove it. Pull your pants down and point out the area where it was inserted." I did as he asked, mortified of him seeing my ass.

"It was put right here." I pointed to the spot.

"Okay, honey, this is going to hurt like a motherfucker with no meds," he said.

"It's okay, James. I'm used to pain. Please remove it." I gritted my teeth as he used the scalpel to open my cheek. He dug around until he found it and removed it. He handed it to me.

"Oh, this is some weird shit," he said. I laughed and put the chip on the floor and stomped on it. I went to the bathroom and threw my phone in the toilet.

"Thank you, James. I owe you."

I left as quickly as I could. I went to an ATM as close as I could and withdrew enough money for tonight. I would go to the bank tomorrow and remove a few thousand to get by and go in the hiding. My heart hurt so badly. How could I ever be so stupid to believe someone could want me and love me? I walked as fast as I could. I pulled my hoodie over my head as I walked the street. I hailed a taxi and headed to the bus station. I kept my hoodie up and got a ticket for Texas. The bus would be here in fifteen minutes. From Texas, I'd grab a rental car or something to California. I loaded the bus and made my way to the last seat in the back. I tried to relax. As soon as the bus started moving, I took a deep breath in and prayed I was going to be okay.

Angelino

I got a phone call in the middle of a conversation with Annika. She was upset about something. My ex, Jessica, called in a panic and said she was in trouble. She was in Indianapolis at a hotel and said she had been raped. I left Annika standing there to help Jessica. I hated people who hurt women. It took me three hours to get there. Before I headed up to check on her, I sent Annika a text.

> Me: I won't be home tonight. I'm sleeping at the
>   penthouse.
> Annika: Okay...do you want me to come there
>   to be with you?
> Me: No need. I'll be home tomorrow. Good
>   night.
> Annika: Be safe. I love you, good night.

I headed up to the hotel room and knocked. She opened the door looking like she was ready to walk the runway.

"Are you okay?" I asked Jessica.

"I'm great, now that you're here," she said in a seductive voice.

"Were you raped, or did you use that to get me here?"

"I had to get you away from that pathetic wife of yours. I know she can't make you happy like I can." Then my phone rang.

"What is it, brother?" I said.

"Where are you? Vera said she heard Annika sobbing in her room. What's going on?"

"Fuck," I said. "I won't be home tonight. I'm out of town."

"You're not coming home? Annika is going to be upset," Giovanni said to me.

"Come on, baby. Let me make you come," Jessica said as loud as she could for Giovanni to hear.

"Who's the woman I hear? Is that Jessica? What the hell are you doing, brother?" Giovanni said. Then I heard breaking glass over the phone. "God, Annika, are you okay?" Giovanni asked my wife.

"I'm…I'm…sorry," I heard Annika say.

"What's going on, Giovanni?" I asked.

"Your wife overheard my conversation. She knows you're with Jessica. She knocked over a vase when she stumbled and cut her hands open. She doesn't look too good. She looks very upset."

"Jesus Christ, how the hell could you let her hear our conversation?" I yelled at him.

"Me? You stupid fuck! She's the best thing that's ever happened to you, and you fucking blew it over a whore. This is on you, brother," he said. He hung up on me.

I rubbed my hand over my face. I cancelled a date with my wife to come run to a stupid bitch who didn't even need help. How could this night get any worse?

I turned to Jessica. "Don't ever call me again, even if you're dying," I said to her and left the hotel room.

I got to the car and tried to call Annika. It went straight to voice mail. She turned her phone off. Of course, what the hell was I thinking? Giovanni called me thirty minutes later.

"What?" I said.

"Your wife left," Giovanni finally said.

"What do you mean, left?"

"She left with the driver, and she took her bodyguards to go out to an all-night restaurant," he said.

"She probably just needed to get out of the house. Contact me when she gets home. I'll be home in a couple hours." I hung up.

Another thirty minutes went by, and one of Annika's bodyguards called.

"What's going on?" I said.

"Your wife ditched us at a restaurant. She went to the bathroom and snuck out of the bathroom window," he said.

"Are you kidding me? You can't keep up with the little woman? Find her now!" I screamed and hung up the phone. I called Luca.

"Yes, boss," he said.

"I need you to track Annika now!"

"On it. She is in an apartment on Fifteenth Street. She has been there for fifteen minutes. I'm sending you the address now," he said.

I sent the info to the guards and then headed that way. Another fifteen minutes and Luca called back.

"What's up?" I said.

"Her GPS just went offline, along with her phone," he said.

"How the hell is that even possible? I need to her found now!" I panicked at this point. "Whatever it takes," I said. "Call my brother and get a team on this. I'm a couple hours out."

"I'll find her," he said.

I finally made it back to the house. Giovanni was sitting on the stairs in the foyer with his hands over his face.

"She went to a friend's house she went to medical school with, and he removed the tracker. She crushed it and threw her phone in the toilet. She can't be tracked like that anymore. She doesn't want to be found, Angelino. You hurt her more than once today, and she's already been broken," Giovanni said.

I stood there and looked at him. What the hell had I done? She ran from me, and she was crying when I left her. It broke her when she knew I was with Jessica. I felt sick. She trusted me, and I broke it. I could only imagine what she was thinking.

"How am I going to find her? Hello, yes, Luca," I said, answering my phone.

"She used an ATM right down the street and withdrew $500. I did face recognition software and caught her on a camera heading into a bus station. She paid in cash, but she was headed to Dallas, Texas," Luca said.

"How far of a lead does she have?"

Luca replied, "Three hours. She'll be on the bus another eleven hours."

"Fuel the jet. I need to get to her now," I said.

"On it," Luca said.

I looked at Giovanni, who was glaring at me.

"I didn't go to sleep with Jessica. She called and said she needed help. That she had been raped," I said to him.

"That's what the police are for. You left your upset wife, canceling a date to run to an ex-girlfriend? Angelino, do you even love Annika?" he asked.

"Of course, I do," I said.

"Well, you're not acting like it. You put your ex before your wife. She's probably one of the most amazing women I've ever met, and you just crushed her. She deserves so much better than that. She worships you, and you cast her aside like she's nothing. You need to really ask yourself if you really love her or if you're just using her," he said, walking off.

My heart sank to my stomach. My heart, my precious wife. What was I thinking? I was thinking I needed to get away from her because I had two months' worth of blue balls.

I headed to the airport, landed in Dallas, and grabbed a cab for the bus station. Luca called.

"Your wife got off the bus in another town and disappeared. I can't find her."

"Please stay on it. I need her home," I said. *She is too smart for her own good*, I thought to myself. I stayed where I was at until I found out where she was headed. Fourteen hours later, they still couldn't find her. I was losing my mind. I called Luca. "Anything?"

"Wait. She just withdrew $5,000 from the account in a small town in Texas," Luca said.

I got back on the jet and landed outside the small town. It was too small to have a cab company. "Where are you headed, Bella?" I said to myself. I got a text from Luca.

> Luca: Cameras pick her up at a truck stop 50 miles from me.
> Me: I need a chopper here now!
> Luca: I'll have one there shortly.

Half an hour later, I landed at the truck stop. I asked a dozen people if they had seen the woman in the picture.

"She came in with a truck driver. But she didn't leave with anyone. I've not seen her since," the waitress said.

"Is there a hotel or anything around here?"

"There are cabins to rent outside town. Here's the address," she said.

"Is there a car rental place or something around?" I asked.

"Yes, a block from here."

I headed down and rented an ugly ass car, the only thing they had left. Then I headed to the address. There were four cabins sitting on the lake. The driveway came around the lake, and I could see the back of the cabins. I parked the car and walked through the trees to look at the cabin to see if I could see anything.

She was here. Thank God. She was sitting on the steps with her head on her knees. She was sobbing. Jesus, I did that to her. My poor Bella. I walked around the lake and walked up to the cabin.

"Bella?" I said. She jerked up fast and saw me.

"Oh my god," she said. She stood up and started backing away. Her hands were wrapped. Giovanni said she cut herself.

"How...how did you find me?" she said in a trembling voice.

Why was she scared of me? I never physically hurt her.

"It wasn't easy to find you," I said. I started walking up the stairs, and she continued to back up.

"Annika, stop moving," I said to her.

She stopped and dropped her gaze to her feet. She was taking in panic breaths. She looked like she had seen a ghost. She leaned against the wall she was standing next to and slid down the wall to her knees. I walked slowly over to her, not wanting to scare her any more.

"Please...please, Angelino, make it fast, please. Please don't make me suffer," she said as tears rolled down her cheeks.

Oh my god, she thinks I'm going to kill her or torture her. Jesus, how this got so bad. I dropped down to my knees in front of her. I put my head to hers.

"God, Bella, I would never hurt you. I just came to bring you home. You think I would hurt you?" I asked her.

She nodded. "Because I left, and this is a crime in the Mafia. I know I would be killed if I was found," she said.

"I love you. I can't believe you thought I'd hurt you."

"I'm nobody, and now I have embarrassed you," she said.

"Why do you say you're a nobody?"

"You married me to get back at my father. I should have known. You're too good to be true. You're just using me like you said to make my father suffer. But I am nothing, Angelino. No one will suffer for me. That explains why don't desire or want me. I'm not…I'm not…" She couldn't get the words out. She was so upset.

I stood and picked her up in my arms. I carried her to the cabin and found the bed. I lay her down on the bed and held her next to me until she was calm enough to talk.

"Bella, I am not using you. My feelings are real. I swear to God. I only want you as my wife or anything else. I don't want anyone but you. Please believe me." She said nothing. "Talk to me," I said to her.

"I'm sorry. I'll be a better wife. Whatever you want, I'll do, Angelino. What do I need to do?"

"I don't understand this. You're perfect. I don't want you to do anything."

She said nothing else. I knew she was thinking about something. Why was she talking about this and not about Jessica?

"Are you upset because I went to see Jessica?" I asked her.

She took a deep breath. "No. I understand." That was all she said.

"Then why did you leave?" I asked her.

"I don't belong there. I'll never be enough for you. I love Grazia, but I want…" She ended the sentence.

"What, Annika? What do you want?"

"My own life, where I can count on myself," she said. My heart was in my shoes.

"You don't want to be with me anymore?" I asked her.

"I love you, but I'm too damaged to be what you need and want. I realized it before you left. I know I will never be what you need or want. And this marriage is for life. I know you will have mistresses and move on with your life. I can't see you with anyone else. It will kill me."

"Please, Bella, you're breaking my heart. How can you want me one day and then you don't the next?" I asked her.

"I do want you. I've been practically begging you for weeks. You don't want me. Even though it hurts, Angelino, I understand it. I know why you left me the other night and why you want to be with Jessica. But it doesn't make it hurt any less. I just wish I never fell in love with you," she said with tears falling down her face.

"Baby girl, I've wanted you since the day I met you. I've wanted every inch of you."

"You won't even let me touch you. Like I'm dirty or something. I hate how it feels when you push me away. And then you run to another woman."

I flipped her on her back and lay on top of her. She wouldn't look at me. "You're not dirty or damaged. I didn't mean to hurt you. I was trying to protect you. You have been through so much, and I don't know how to proceed with that. I feel like I'm taking advantage of you. Please look at me. I'm so sorry for everything. Please give me a chance to fix this. Don't shut me out. I need you."

She opened her eyes.

"I should have never left the other night. I left because Jessica told me she was raped. But that's not an excuse, Bella. I should have never left you. I was scared if I stayed, I would go too far with you and hurt you. I should have stayed. Please, Bella, I don't want anyone else in my heart or in my bed, and I swear to God I will never put anybody before you again. I love you so much," I begged her. My heart hurt.

"I love you too," she said.

"You forgive me? Do you really want to be without me?"

"I forgive you, Angelino. No, it just hurt you not wanting to be with me. And you would rather have been with Jessica than me," she said.

"I've wanted to be with you. You drive me crazy. And the last person I want is Jessica. She does not come close to you," I said.

"I'm not going to break. I need you to replace all the negative I've been through, Angelino, with us. I need that so much," she said.

What an idiot I had been. She needed me to be with her, and I was trying to keep her safe.

"I'm sorry, Annika. Please come home," I said to her.

"I will," she said.

"Thank God," I said. "My family's fucking mad as hell at me for hurting you. They will kill me if I come home without you." She smiled up at me, almost like she didn't believe I wanted her.

I leaned down and kissed her softly. We explored each other's mouths. She was holding back. I could feel it. She was afraid.

I kissed down her neck, and she moaned. I pressed my hard dick between her legs. My dick was going to explode in my jeans.

"Do you see what you do to me? Do you feel that?" I asked her.

I continued to dry hump her until we were both moaning. I sat up and pulled her dress over her head. She had no bra on. I leaned down and sucked one of her nipples.

"Oh god," she whispered.

I pulled my clothes off, and she was still in her panties. I moved back between her legs and let my dick lay against her slit as I kissed her neck.

"Please, please," she said.

"What do you need, Bella?"

"You. Always you," she said.

Well, fuck if that didn't touch my heart. I came up beside her and pulled her to me. I reached down and slipped my hand in her panties and started rubbing her clit.

"That feels so good," she said. "Please let me feel you inside me. Please," she begged.

"I promise I will. I just want to take my time." I put two fingers in and started pumping in and out.

"More…I want more." I pulled my fingers out and lined my dick with her slit.

"Look at me, Bella," I said. She opened her eyes, her nails digging in my arms.

"You tell me to stop if you need to and I'll stop."

"Okay. Please, Angel, let me feel you in me. I need this."

I slipped in a little at a time.

"God, you're so tight!" I said through gritted teeth. I moved slowly in and out until I was fully seated. She wrapped her legs around my back, giving me a deeper angle. I leaned down until I was almost laying on her. I took her mouth with passion. She started meeting my strokes. She ran her nails down my back.

"I'm going to come!" she screamed as her walls clamped around me.

God, she was killing me. I slowed down before I lost it. I flipped us over and put her on top.

"You're gorgeous. Ride me. Come again all over me."

"Talk to me," she said.

She likes that, does she? "Does my dick feel good, Bella?"

"Yes, God, yes."

"I love feeling your wet pussy on my cock." She moaned loudly and started moving faster.

"Your pussy is so tight. It's just made for me. Is your pussy going to come all over my dick?"

"Oh, Angelino!" she screamed my name as her orgasm hit her.

I grabbed her hips and started pumping into her fast and hard.

"Feels so good." I let out my release with a bellow. She collapsed on my chest. I kissed her head.

"You're so amazing. I love you, Bella. You are my life." She kissed my chest.

"I love you so much it hurts."

We lay there until we both fell asleep. I woke up, and she was not in bed.

"Oh shit," I said, scrambling out of bed. Then I heard the water running. She was taking a shower. She didn't leave. I walked in the bathroom. She was in the shower.

"May I join you?"

"I would love that," she said.

I stepped in. She acted like she was going to touch me and stopped herself.

"Bella, I'm sorry I ever made you stop when you wanted to touch me. I swear I was just trying to go slow with you. I was scared I would hurt you. Please don't hold back. I'm yours to touch whenever you want. Please, Bella."

She tucked her hair behind her ears, walked over to me, wrapped her arms around me, and kissed my chest. She licked my left nipple, and it went straight to my cock. She reached down and grabbed my cock. She stroked it slowly.

"Bella, that feels good."

She bit my chest lightly. I came undone. I lifted her up, and she wrapped her arms around my neck and her legs around my waist. I pressed her against the shower wall and pushed my cock all the way in until I was balls deep in one stroke. She gasped.

"Fuck me, Angel, please."

"Bella, you drive me crazy." I fucked her hard in the shower.

"Yes, yes, Angelino!" she screamed as she came, and I was right behind her.

"Fuck, Bella!" I bellowed as I came. I stayed there for a minute, kissing her roughly. I pulled back and looked at her. "You're so perfect."

"So are you."

I let her down, and we finished showering. We both dressed and headed to the kitchen. She made some coffee and sats on the barstool in front of me.

"I'm sorry I ran," she said.

"It's okay. It's my fault. If I wasn't such an idiot. You can trust me, I promise. Her number has been blocked, Bella. I'm sorry I hurt you. You mean everything to me. I was going crazy without you. Promise me you'll never leave me again," I said.

"I won't," she said as she stared down at her lap.

"Are you ready to go home?" I asked her.

"I am," she said.

We drank our coffee and grabbed her bag and walked around the lake to my car. She looked at the car and then at me and then started laughing.

"It's all they had." I laughed along with her.

We dropped off the car and walked toward the diner.

"Where are we going?" she asked.

"To the chopper. It's in the parking lot," I said.

"I figured you would take the jet," she said.

"I did twice, but you kept moving, and it was easier. This is our call for a chopper," I said.

"You went through all that for me?" she asked.

"God, yes, Bella. I told you, you're everything to me. I will always come for you." She smiled at me, and we got in that chopper and headed home.

The chopper landed on the beach behind our house. Vera, Giovanni, and Amelia were waiting in the garden. Giovanni looked relieved, and he walked up to her and embraced her. That kind of shocked me. He was not a loving guy. He pulled back from her.

"I'm so glad you're home. I was worried sick," he said.

"I'm sorry I worried you," she said as she put her head down.

We headed back to the house. I wanted to stay close to Annika for a couple of days. I needed her to know how much she meant to me.

"What do you want to do today?" I asked.

"I was thinking of going shopping. I want to furnish the library, and I think I want some more clothes. If that's good with you," she said.

Clothes took me off guard. She always looked beautiful, but she never asked for much.

"I would love to take you shopping," I said. She raised an eyebrow at me.

"Then we can go eat somewhere," I said to her.

"That sounds great."

I had the car brought around, and we headed to the furniture store. She ordered a huge rectangular table about twenty foot long with armed wing chairs to go around it. The table was white, and the chairs were gray with blues throughout. She ordered a huge area rug, then some love seats, lamps, and some end tables.

Then we headed to Stilettos, a high-end women's store.

"Enjoy yourself, Bella. I'm going sit right here," I told her.

She took her time walking around. She had put on some weight and looked healthier and sexier. I couldn't wait to see what she got. One of the dress assistants helped her as she walked around. She picked out several dresses and clothes. The assistant took shoes in her size to her.

I heard the bell ring over the door, and in walked Jessica. What the fuck. I stood up, and she looked at me.

"Wow, fancy meeting you here," she said.

"Did you follow me here?" I asked her.

Because I was so focused on Annika, I really wasn't looking for threats.

"You left in such a hurry, and my calls are not getting through. So I came to talk to you."

"I blocked you for a reason, Jessica. The whole rape thing was not cool. You and I are done. I told you I don't want anything to do with you."

She stepped closer. There was only an inch between us, and she put her hands on my arm.

"Oh, you don't mean that," she said in a seductive voice.

Before I could reply, Annika grabbed her wrists, removing her from my arm. She stepped between us. Annika was in a tight blue pencil dress that came right above her knee, and she was in four-inches stilettos with her hair pulled up in a tight high ponytail. Damn, she looked fierce. She was a couple of inches taller than Jessica. Jessica was no match for Annika's beauty, and she knew it.

"My husband made himself quite clear. But that has not seemed to deter you. So let me make myself very clear. Do not come near or try to contact my husband. I don't take kindly to someone messing with my family. I will end you. Are we fucking clear?" she told her.

Holy shit, my Bella was dropping the F bomb. And in a Russian accent.

"What…what, are you threatening me?" Jessica asked.

"I am a Russian Mafia princess and an Italian Mafia queen. I will take your life and not even think twice about it. Remove yourself from our lives, or I'll do it for you, Jessica," Annika said.

Jessica was physically shaken. She was fucking scared. She backed away and ran out the door.

"Shit, that was so hot. I almost came on myself, Annika." What was happening? She was radiating power. She turned around and put her arms around my neck. She looked in my eyes and then kissed me.

She pulled back and said, "Do you like my dress?" She winked at me.

"I love that fucking dress and your attitude in it. I just want to back you into the wall and screw you senseless!"

"Maybe we can arrange that," she said, and I laughed.

"We will try it when we get home. We have a day of shopping. Please continue getting anything you want. I'm so turned on right now." She laughed as she walked off.

She headed back to the dressing room. She left the blue dress on and the heels, and we checked out a ton of clothes, shoes, and handbags. I had them delivered to the house. We stopped at Monta Chu Chus, a high-end shoe designer. She picked out about twenty pairs of shoes, and we continued to different stores. We stepped into a boutique that specialized in lingerie. I picked out several things I loved, and she got several bras sets. We had those delivered to the house.

"What would you like to eat?" I asked her.

"Somewhere quiet that has music."

"I know the perfect place. It's a little hole-in-the-wall. It's in our territory and owned by one of the people my father used to strong-arm. The food is amazing."

We headed to Giorgio's. As we walked in, a young girl said, "Mr. Rossi, we were not expecting you. Let me get my father."

I laughed because they were still scared after what my father did to them.

"Mr. Rossi, it's so nice to see you. How I may help you?" the older gentleman said as he walked in.

"Mr. Romano, it's great to see you again. This is my beautiful wife, Annika. I've been telling her how amazing your food is here. Can we get a table somewhere quiet?"

He relaxed. "Absolutely. Follow me."

He took us to a table toward the back in a sectioned-off area. We had the room to ourselves.

"How is this?" he asked.

"Perfect. When does the band play?"

"They will be back in a few minutes. They went on break. Can I start you off with some wine or bread?"

"I would love a bottle of dark Dom Pérignon. If you carry it. We are celebrating, and it calls for champagne, I told him.

"If we don't have it, we will go get it. I'll be right back with your bread."

"This place is nice."

"I thought you might like it. My brother and I are trying to help our people. Eating at the restaurants and using and shopping at their stores. It helps put money back into our community, but it also brings them more business."

"Mafia heroes," she said, laughing.

"Something like that," I said, laughing.

Mr. Ramiro brought out our champagne and poured us each a glass. I looked at her and raised my glass.

"To new beginnings and my fierce wife," I said. She giggled and raised her glass.

"Oh, this is so good," she said, taking a sip.

Mr. Ramiro came back. "Do you want to order now?"

"What would you like?" I asked Annika.

"Do you mind ordering for me? You know what is great here," she said to me.

"If you would like, Mr. and Mrs. Rossi, I can arrange several small dishes for you to try," the owner said.

"I would love that," Annika said.

"Then that's a yes," I said to him.

"What's happening in the business world?" Annika asked.

"We are making plans to end your father in the next few months. Are you okay with that?"

"Yes, his reign needs to end."

"We are going to take the rest of his money. Since I married you, everything we have taken from him is an account for you. Everything that's his will be yours."

"Ours. It will be ours, Angelino. We are a team. I'd rather you invest it. I'm a doctor, not a businesswoman."

"I can invest it for you. I'll let you know where it goes."

"Thank you. I would like to invest some of it in some kind of kid's program to help with dyslexia with free tutors or something. And something for medical. I'm not sure what yet."

"We'll think about it, and we will make it happen." Our food came, and it was amazing.

"Mr. Ramiro, the food is amazing," Annika said.

"Thank you, Mrs. Rossi. That means a lot." I handed them the credit card to pay the bill.

"No need, sir. It's on the house," he said.

"I really appreciate that, Mr. Ramiro, but my family and I are not here to take advantage of our people. We bring our business to you because we want to help you grow," I said to him. I put the card back in my wallet because I knew he was not going charge me for the $500 bottle of champagne. I pulled out $1,000 in cash and put it on the table.

"Thank you for the amazing food, Mr. Ramiro. You're worth every penny," I said as Annika and I got up and headed out the door.

"I love you," she said.

"I love you too, Bella." I kissed her.

We got back to the house, and all the bags had been delivered. She looked through them quickly and grabbed the bag she was looking for.

"What's that?" I asked.

"Some princess dresses and tiaras for Grazia. She likes to dress up."

I smile at her for taking care of Grazia.

"I'll have the staff take the rest to our room," I said to her.

"Thank you."

"I have some work that needs to be done. I'll meet you later, and we'll have a family dinner," I said, kissing her lips. She smiled and walked upstairs to Grazia. About an hour later, she knocked on my office door. My door was open.

"You don't have to knock. This is your office too."

"Can I talk to you about something?" she asked.

"Anything. What's on your mind? Come here sit on my lap." She sat in my lap.

"I want Grazia to be mine," she said.

"She is yours, Bella."

"I want to adopt her. To make it official."

"You do?

"Yes. I want her as my own," she said.

"I think Grazia will love that."

"We can throw her a huge party to celebrate. What do you think?" she said.

"Yes. I'll call our lawyer and have the papers done ASAP! Thank you for this." I kissed her softly. "My mother's coming back tomorrow. Fair warning."

"I can't wait," she said in a sarcastic tone.

"Don't worry. I'll take care of anything she throws at you," I said. She kissed my lips and got up, and we would meet for dinner.

We met up later and enjoyed our meal. We headed to our room after Annika tucked in Grazia. She walked out on the terrace, where I was seated. She was in a nightgown with skinny straps in a champagne color. It came right above her knee. Hell, she was sexy. She came over and sat on my lap.

"What are you thinking about?" she asked.

"Just what an amazing woman you are. My entire family is under your spell," I told her.

She laughed out loud. She leaned down and kissed me. And it turned hungry between us. She sat sideways in my lap with her back to my left arm. She removed my hand from her face and pulled back.

"Angelino, please touch me," she said as she put my hand between her legs.

"Damn, Bella, no panties?"

She smiled at me. This little vixen knew what she was doing to me.

141

I rubbed her clit softly and fast until she was panting.

"Finger me, please, Angel." I did what she asked.

I put two fingers in her and moved in and out slowly.

"Faster, oh god." I leaned up to get a better angle.

I finger fucked her hard as she had her legs spread wide in my lap. I could hear the wet smacking noises of my fingers slapping into her. She was moaning loudly.

"You like me finger fucking you, Bella? Do you like it hard? You're going to come on my fingers?"

And with that, she screamed, "Yes, god, yes, I'm coming!" She spasmed around my fingers.

As she settled, she stood up and removed her nightgown. I watched her to see what she was going to do next. She got more confident every day, and I wanted to feed that. She reached down and started pulling my boxers down. I lifted my hips so she could get them off all the way down. She sat in my lap with both legs hanging over the armrest so her pussy was on my lap. She reached in and kissed me roughly. I rubbed her nipple, and she moaned. She raised herself up and slid my big cock inside her.

"You feel so good," I told her.

She braced her hands on the armrests and used it to lift herself up and down on my cock.

I growled. "You're so tight."

We were not making love. We were fucking. It was animalistic. I put my hands on her hips and slammed her down hard on my cock. I lifted my hips up from the chair to meet her. Our bodies slapped together hard.

"Angel, you feel so good. Please fuck me harder, Angelino," she said. I slammed her down on my dick, and she screamed. I fucked her hard and rough.

Her walls started to tighten around me, and we both exploded at the same time. We were both sweating and panting.

"I love you so much," she said.

"I love you too. You do things to me no woman can," I said to her.

I held her for several minutes. Then we headed to the shower and then to bed. She curled up next to me and put an arm and a leg over me. I ran my fingers down her back until she fell asleep. I tried to sleep, but I knew my mother would bring hell with her when she came, and I must be able to protect her.

Annika

Things between Angelino and I had been amazing. He had been spending a lot of time with me. His mother came in today, and I worried about the way she'd treat me. But with Angelino's help, I got more confident every day.

We went shopping yesterday because I wanted to look beautiful for him. It gave me confidence wearing clothes that made me feel beautiful.

Angelino was still asleep. I watched him. He was so gorgeous with his long lashes and a body of a god. I slipped down and put his cock in my mouth. He started getting hard immediately. His hands went to my hair.

"God, Bella," he moaned.

I stroked his long thick shaft with my hand as I licked and sucked the head of his dick. I moved his dick as far back in my throat as I could get.

"Yes, I like when you suck it like that," he growled in a husky voice.

He gently started shoving my head down on his cock.

"I'm going to come if you don't stop," he said in a husky voice. But I didn't stop. I picked up my pace as he hollered out. When he came, he hit the back of my throat, and I swallowed all of it. I licked it all off his dick. He looked down at me.

"Holy shit, woman. That was erotic as hell waking up like that," he said, breathing hard.

I hovered over him and kissed him softly.

"I love you."

"Love you too." I got up.

"Where are you going? I haven't touched you yet." I smiled at him.

"It was all about you this morning," I said. He smiled at me. "Come on, sexy. Let's go eat breakfast. We have a party to plan for the adoption celebration on Saturday," I said to him.

"You're excited, aren't you?"

"Yes." I was happy Grazia was just as excited. "The lawyer is bringing the papers over today to make it official, right?" I asked him.

"Yes. He will be here at noon. My mother will be here around two," he said, rolling his eyes.

"I can't wait," I said, winking at him. He laughed.

I wore a floral print split leg dress with a white plain wedge sandal. I put my hair half up in curls. I looked sexy but casual. I stepped out of the bathroom.

"You're going be the death of me dressing like that." I laughed.

"Then I guess I'm doing something right."

"Oh, you are, Bella. You do everything right."

He was in black slacks and a white button-down shirt.

"You keep dressing like that, and we won't make it out of this room," I said to him.

"Then I guess my plan is working." We both laughed.

We headed down to breakfast. We went by Grazia's room and walked her down. We ate breakfast, and Angelino went to his office to take care of business. Grazia headed to the playground with Mari.

I headed to the library to see that things were coming along. The room had tall forty-foot ceilings with old murals painted on them. Bookcases covered the walls all the way to the ceiling. They were stairs leading up to the walkway along the walls. It was dark and gloomy. I wanted warm and inviting. I didn't do anything drastic. I added lighter colored drapes and furniture and several seating areas along the long table so anyone could lay material out to study. I added some pictures of Angelino and his two brothers to the walls in black and white. And it looked great.

"Mr. Rossi wants you in his office," Vera said.

"Thank you. I'm headed that way now." I went into his office and walked in.

"Hey, Bella, are you ready to sign the papers?" he asked as his lawyer laid the papers on the desk.

"Yes, I am." We both signed all the paperwork that he pushed through, and I was officially Grazia's mother. I teared up, and Angelino came over and kissed my head.

"You're such an amazing woman," he said.

"I'm headed to the courthouse to file these. Is there anything else you need, sir?" the lawyer said.

"Not at this time. Thank you again." And he left.

"I have something for you," Angelino said.

"You do?" He handed me a velvet box. I opened it. It was a platinum charm bracelet. It had two charms. One had a heart that said, "Greatest Mother Ever." One was a picture of him and us on our wedding day.

"It's so beautiful. This means so much," I told him.

"We can add to it as we grow together."

"Thank you so much," I said.

His phone rang.

"Hey, Giovanni. We will be down shortly." He hung up.

"Mother's here early," he said as he let out a long breath. I grabbed his face.

"It's going to be okay. We will get through this together," I said. He smiled.

"You're right. Let's go." As we make our way to the foyer, Giovanni came from the kitchen to meet up with us.

"Where is Amelia?" I asked.

"I'm not letting Satan get her claws on her. She's too innocent," he said.

I looked at Angelino and gave him a reassuring wink. We opened the front door. A short plump woman was standing there. She gave Angelino and Giovanni a huge smile.

"My boys," she said.

Okay, maybe she was not so bad. They grabbed their mother's bags. Not even a hug between them. They walked into the house.

She did not even see me because she was too busy looking at the foyer. It had completely changed.

"Who the hell destroyed the foyer? Where's all the art that was on the walls? This is not staying like this. I want it back the way it was!" she screamed.

Okay, maybe not so nice, I thought to myself. Angelino put my arm through his and walked me over to his fuming mother.

"Mother," Angelino said. She turned to look at us.

"Who the hell is she? What is she doing in my house?" she said.

Angelino took a deep breath. "So this is how you want to play this? Because Giovanni and I have had enough over our lifetime. This fucking house is ours, not yours. So get that straight. You're only here because we allow it." Angelino was seething.

"This has always been my house. I'm in charge of it!" she yelled.

"Enough!" Giovanni yelled at her. "Keep your mouth shut for a fucking second and Angelino will explain things to you." She just stood there and stared at Angelino. She was pissed.

"Mother, this is Annika. She is my wife. She is now in charge of the house," Angelino said.

"Nice to meet you," I said, hanging on to Angelino.

"You married some Russian dog? What the hell is wrong with you?"

He released me and grabbed his mother by the throat.

"Apologize right now or I will snap your damn neck," he said through gritted teeth.

"I apologize," she said in a whisper. Angelino stayed where he was.

"Here are how things are going to play out, Mother. Listen well, because I'm only saying it once. Annika is my wife. She is the head of this house. She is my queen. She is also Grazia's mother. You will show her respect, and you will keep your fucking mouth shut, or I will ship you back to your sisters with no support. Or I can end your pathetic life after I cut your tongue out," he said.

She was not used to her sons being so dominant.

She nodded.

"Good. Get out of my face," he said.

She grabbed her bags and headed to the stairs to her room.

I put my hand on Angelino's arm, trying to calm him.

"Well, that went well," I said, laughing. They both started laughing with me.

"Thank you for not playing into that," Angelino said to me.

"You're welcome. I love you. It'll all be okay," I said to him, kissing him on his cheek.

The next couple of days went by as usual. His mother joined us for breakfast and didn't say anything. She gave me nasty look anytime the brothers were not watching. She did not worry me. I lived my whole life with a bully. And that was exactly what she was. A bully. Grazia stayed away from her.

"Mommy, after breakfast, can we go swimming?" Grazia asked me.

"Of course, we can," I said.

"You allow your daughter to call her Mother already?" his mother asked.

Angelino looked up at the end of the table. "I did not allow anything. Grazia asked her if she could, and she is her mother. She adopted Grazia. I don't want to hear anything else about it."

"Where is Salvatore? He wasn't here yesterday. I'd like to say hello."

"He's guarding the perimeter. He no longer has a seat at the table, and good luck with trying to get him to say anything back. I cut his fucking tongue out," Angelino said. She did not say anything else. She knew she could be next.

A few days later, I was sitting in the library and reading a book when his mother came in.

Oh, this is going to be interesting, I thought to myself. She did not see me at first. I was in the corner. She walked around and stared at all the new furniture and pictures.

"Russian whore," I heard her say. I laughed to myself.

"Well, hello to you too," I said, bringing her attention back to me. She glared at me and then looked around and made sure we were alone.

"You walk in here so high and mighty. You think you're the queen? You're nothing. You're dirt under my shoe. You're a Russian dog. You'll pay for being here. I'll make sure of it," she said.

I laughed then said, "I look forward to it."

I was done with her theatrics. She glared at me and walked out. Every time we were alone, she had something nasty to say. I could tell Angelino, but I was trying to stand my ground without playing her games.

Angelino

"We need to move forward with our plan and take down Volkov permanently. He is pushing for a war with the Greeks, and we both don't want that," I said to my brother.

"I will get with Luca and have him take the rest of his money. He shifted his accounts and thinks they're safe," Giovanni said.

"Good. Let's get Salvatore and all his top men to start making them disappear, including all their foot soldiers. Make sure we know all his safe houses."

"I'll get on that immediately. I want to take Amelia out to our house in Colorado to do some hiking and relax in nature. We wanted to take Grazia with us," Giovanni said.

"That's a great idea, and Grazia would love it. That would give Annika a couple days of rest. She has not been feeling well. She threw up a couple times."

"Is she pregnant?" Giovanni asked.

"No, she can't be. The contraceptive still has like five to six months left on it, and the doctor told her that it could be another six months after that."

"We would love more babies running around here," Giovanni said.

"I plan on it. Annika starts her residency soon. She would look so hot with a swollen belly and a lab coat." We both started laughing. "I'm headed to the warehouse to check on our shipments. I guess I'll see you in a few days," I said.

"See you, brother."

I headed out to the warehouse and checked everything. We did our rounds every week to check on our people and our investments. After the warehouse, I stopped by several of the stores to check on our people. Most seemed to be doing well. I stepped into a pastry shop. There were no customers inside. There were no pastries of any kind either. I heard arguing in the back.

"You can't quit college. It's your way out of here," I heard a woman say.

"I don't have a choice, Ma. We can't afford college, and now the shop is closed. I must get a job," a male voice said.

"Hello," I said loudly.

"I'm sorry. We are closed," said the woman as she came around from the back. "Oh, Mr. Rossi. How are you?"

"Mrs. Bruno, how are you?" I said.

"We are good. Thank you," she said.

"I overheard your conversation. What's going on with the shop?" I asked.

She reluctantly answered, "The electrical that goes to our ovens is fried."

"How long before you're back up?" I asked.

"We are going to have to close shop. The electrical is the landlord's responsibility, and he refuses to pay to fix it. He says it's our fault, and I must pay the $20,000 to replace it."

"Enzo, son, come out here please," I said. He stood beside his mother. He was about twenty.

"What are you going to college for?"

"I'm getting my architectural degree," he said.

"Amazing profession. I can't wait to see what you accomplish. Contact me when you get out of college. We could use an architect if you're interested," I said. His mother looked worried. "We would have all our legitimate businesses though. I would keep you clean. But it's just an offer."

"Well, I won't be finishing. I must drop out to work. We won't make it if I don't," Enzo said, and his mother had tears in her eyes.

"You're not dropping out of college. I'll pay for your college in full, and the building will be repaired by the end of the week. I'll have some cash brought over to last the rest of the week," I said to both.

"We can't accept that. We will never be able to pay you back," she said nervously.

"Let's be honest, Mrs. Bruno. We owe you for all the money my father strong-armed from you over the years. I'm just settling a debt," I told her.

She seemed happy with that answer.

"Thank you, Mr. Rossi. We appreciate the help. You're a great man," she said. I smiled at her and handed her my card.

"I'll get my people on this. Any other issue, just give me a call," I told her.

"Hey, boss," Matteo said, answering the phone.

"Hey, cuz, I need you to investigate the buildings along Fourteenth Street. I want us to own them and have them brought up-to-date. Here is one I need done by the end of the week. The electrical needs to be repaired. Also, I need $12,000 taken to Mrs. Bruno and her son's college to be paid for in full," I told him.

"Send me the address and I'll have it taken care of," he said.

"Done. Thank you."

I headed home. It would be dinner soon. I wanted some one-on-one time with my beautiful wife. I walked into the house, and it was too quiet. Probably because Grazia was gone. I walked around the house. The chef was making dinner. The guards were all on post. I walked everywhere that I knew Annika would be. I started calling her phone, and as I made it to our room again, I heard it. It was on the floor by the bed. Something was wrong. I felt it in my bones. I called Luca.

"Can you track Annika? I found her phone, but I can't seem to find her. I'm worried. I injected Annika with another chip."

"Yes, let me check. She is in the house. Let me narrow it down. She is in your room," he said.

I walked around the bed and even looked under it. I walked into the bathroom, but I noticed a spot of blood on the floor.

"There's blood on the bathroom floor," I said into the phone.

I pulled my weapon even though I knew no one could have gotten past the grounds. I opened the closet door slowly and saw Annika in a heap on the floor. I ran over to her and moved her hair out of her face, trying to see what was going on.

"Bella, I'm here," I said. "Oh god, Luca. I need an ambulance here now. She has been beaten severely."

One eye was swollen shut. She had a broken nose. Her dress was ripped and covered in blood. Her arms were bruised and cut like she was defending herself. She had been stabbed in one of her arms. She was lying in the fetal position.

"Bella, can you hear me? I'm here, baby," I said to her. She moaned. "I'm going to pick you up and get you to the to the bed." I picked her up and pulled her to my chest. "I love you. You're going to be okay."

The guards escorted the medics up. I reached down to hold her hand, but there was a piece of paper folded in her hand. I shoved into my pocket, focusing on her. She had a scarf around one of her wrists. The paramedics removed it. Someone sliced her wrist to make her bleed out slow. She saved herself by tying it.

"Angel?" she said.

"I'm here, baby. We're taking you to the hospital. I'm not leaving you." I rode to the hospital with her, and they rushed her. I paced as my cousin walked in.

"Well, how is she?" Luca asked.

"I don't know. Someone left her for dead. I have not heard anything from the doctor," I said, putting my hands in my pockets. I felt the paper. I pulled it out and opened it.

"What is that?" Luca asked.

"It was in her hand," I said.

You thought you could remove us from our positions, and nothing happened. This Russian dog will never take our place. I tried to take her tongue like you did mine, but the Russian whore would not open her mouth. She will bleed out slowly, and you will suffer for being so weak to fall in love. Her death will bring you war when they think it's you who killed her. And we will make sure Volkov knows all your secrets. We will

end you and your brother and cousins. We will
run the Russian Mafia. Enjoy your fate.

I handed the letter to my cousins. "Salvatore and who else?"
"Focus on your wife. We will handle the rest. Your brother is on
his way back."
I nodded.

Annika

A couple of weeks passed, and everyone was out of the house. Angelino went out to take care of work. I started working out a couple weeks ago and headed down to the gym and worked out for about an hour. I got this with a wave of nausea and ran to the locker room and threw up.

"Why am I sick all the time?" I asked myself.

I texted, "Can you pick up a couple of pregnancy tests for me?"

Vera replied, "Of course, dear. I'll head out now."

I said, "Thank you. I will be in my room."

I was pretty sure I was not pregnant, but I needed to make sure before I bothered the doctor. I headed to my room and took a cool shower. Vera came up with hot tea and toast, along with the pregnancy tests.

"Thank you, Vera."

"You're very welcome. Are you sure you may be pregnant? You have six months to a year left on your contraceptive. It could be a bug," Vera said.

"No, it is probably a bug of some kind. I don't want to look stupid going to the doctor."

"I'm going to head into town for a bit if you're okay here," Vera said.

"I'm good. I am going to head to the library and read."

Vera headed out. I went to the bathroom and peed on the stick and placed the test on the counter and waited. Two pink lines. I was pregnant. A wave of excitement ran through me. I prayed Angelino was ready. I put the test in the drawer, came out, and drank my tea and ate the toast. I decided to lay down for a bit and ended up falling asleep.

I woke up to a hand over my mouth, and I panicked. My eyes flew open, and Salvatore had his hand pressed down hard on my mouth. He punched me on the left side of my face. He grabbed me by my hair and yanked me out of the bed to the floor. I rolled away from him toward the bathroom. I screamed, but I knew no one would hear me from the back of the castle. He kicked the door open before I could close it.

Fury was flowing off him in waves. He grabbed me by the hair and brought his knee up while bringing my head down, ramming his knee in my face. He shattered my nose, and blood gushed everywhere. I must keep my baby safe. He was going to kill us both. I was so dizzy and disoriented. I fell back through the closet doors and hit the floor. He stalked toward me and started kicking me everywhere. I curled up to protect my stomach, and I put my hands over my head. He kicked and punched me all over my body. He leaned over and grabbed my hair.

He had a knife and moved his hand to my jaw and tried to pry it open. He was going to cut my tongue out. I clenched my jaw tight and started kicking him in the back with my knees. He couldn't hold me still enough alone to cut out my tongue. He brought the knife down in frustration and stabbed me in the arm that I covered my face with. He punched me again, trying to knock me out. But I had been through this several times.

I rolled to my other side. He sliced my left arm, trying to get me to move my arm from my face. He was so pissed and frustrated that he grabbed my hand and sliced me across my wrist. Blood started flowing. He kicked me in the back of the head, and I started to get weaker. He must have been there for a long time, and he put something in my hand and ran out. I reached for a scarf and wrapped it around my wrist tight and collapsed into darkness.

"Bella, I'm here," I heard Angelino say. Thank God he found me.

There was a lot of movement around me, and I was being moved. The next thing I saw were dim lights. I opened my eyes as best as I could. It was dark outside, but I knew I was in the hospital. Angelino was sitting in the chair next to me, holding my hand with his head in my lap. I ran my fingers through his hair, and he looked up at me.

"Thank God, Bella. I was so afraid of losing you."

"I'm way too stubborn to die," I said, and he laughed.

"Yes, you are," he said with a smile.

"How long have I been here?"

"Since yesterday. They had to stop the bleeding on your wrist and repair the ligaments and reconstruct your nose, along with some stitches from a stabbing and a cut you had along your arm."

"I needed a nose job. Did they at least make it smaller?" I said with a smile, trying to lighten the mood.

"You're allowed to be upset, Bella. I've got you."

"You have me. It's why I'm not upset. I've been through this several times. Because of you, I'm no longer a victim. I'm alive. The bruises will fade, and the stitches will be removed. I'll have more scars."

"You're such a warrior, a goddess. Your scars are beautiful just like you," he said and kissed my hand.

"Angel, I need to tell you something, and this is really not the place I wanted to do it."

"What's wrong, Bella?"

"I'm pregnant." I let that sink in. He had tears in his eyes, and he kissed me.

He put his hand on my stomach. Then he jumped up fast and ran to the door.

"I need a doctor here now," he said, and the doctor followed him in.

"My wife is pregnant. I need you to check her to make sure the baby is fine."

"I'll get the sonogram equipment right now," said the doctor, and he left the room.

"I protected our baby. But I do worry about the meds I have running through me."

"I found you in the fetal position. You're a force and selfless. Thank you for protecting our child," he said as he kissed me with tears in his eyes.

The doctor brought in the sonogram equipment. The doctor pulled up my nightgown and put some gel on my stomach. He moved the wand around, and we could hear the heartbeat.

"A very strong heartbeat. You look about two months pregnant. Your baby looks healthy. But when you leave, make sure you set up a panel workup with your ob-gyn," the doctor said.

"What about all the anesthesia and meds they have me on?"

"Women go through things all the time. It should not affect the baby." The nurse took out the equipment.

"Now, Mrs. Rossi, your wrist was damaged pretty bad. You will have full use over it, but you will have stiffness and even some numbness from time to time. We will remove all the stitches in a week if you're healed," the doc said.

"When can I leave?" I asked, and Angelino laughed.

"Tomorrow. You'll also need to check in with a plastic surgeon that operated on your nose."

"I didn't know plastic surgeons did that on an emergency."

"Your husband requested it. He didn't want you to have to go through another surgery," he said and walked out.

I smiled at Angelino. "Thank you."

"Anything for you. Grazi is going to be a big sister. She is going to be as excited as me," he said.

Angelino

I'm going to have another child with the love of my life. Now I need to protect them.

I brought Annika home yesterday. We beefed up security. There were two guards at the main entrance already. But we added guards to each wing of the house and several outside of the room like the library and dining room.

Giovanni came back the night Annika was attacked and worked with our team to find Salvatore and whoever he was working with. The entire Rossi team met in my office. They all took seats around the table.

"A bit of good news before we start business. Annika is pregnant," I said, and the room erupted into congratulations and handshakes.

"I'm so happy for you, brother. You deserve it. How far along is she?" Giovanni asked.

"Two months," I said. "Annika's wrist was severely injured during her attack. She will not be able to be a surgeon. Salvatore took that from her."

"He will pay for it when we find him. I promise you," Giovanni said.

"What is she going to do now?" Dante asked.

"She decided she wanted to be in charge of the clinic Amelia is opening to help our people. They will get free care, and same goes for the medications and surgeries needed. She'll also take in other patients, but at a cut cost. That way, it all balances out. But we will absorb the cost if necessary. Annika wanted to be part of our vision. And I think she has done that," I said.

"You have an amazing wife. I hope I'm so lucky one day," Rocco said.

"I hope all of you are."

"We think we might know who Salvatore is working with," Luca said.

I looked at him. "Who?"

"Your mother," Luca said flatly. Giovanni and I looked at each other.

"If she is, she just signed her death warrant," I said.

"That's not all," Luca said. "The cameras picked up Salvatore meeting with Volkov."

"Then we need to presume Volkov knows some of the secret locations of our weapons. He knows all our operations and the layout of all our buildings. All our security measures," I said.

"What do you want to do now?" Dante asked.

"Until we can prove my mother is involved in this, we have to keep a close eye out on her. She's living under this roof, and we must be aware of anything she may be up to. We also need to come up with a plan to be ahead of Volkov. We need to shut him down before he can start."

"We need to bring in the MC guys to help protect the house and our people. We go after them first."

"He is going to try to take down every business we own," Rocco said.

"I agree. Santos, you contact the MC buddies and see who we can use," I said, and he nodded in agreement.

"I will get Rubble to beef up our firewalls more to keep them out of our security system. I'm sure he is going to try to break through," Luca said.

"Good idea. Salvatore knew of a couple of our business, like the weapons and the strip clubs. And the other properties I got from the alliance," I said.

"I don't think he will mess with the properties from the alliance," Matteo said.

"He will start targeting all of us. He wants us all destroyed so he and probably Mother can run this operation. We start wearing protective vests all the time if we are out," I said.

"I think we need you and your brothers to move in here for now. We can protect all the women better," Giovanni said.

"I agree. I think we need to move the weapons to a new location. I think we need more guards around the clubs, and Luca and Rubble can keep face recognition to run 24-7. We can hire new people, but we will have guards all around," Dante said.

"Now that we have a definite plan, let's work on our offense. I think we need to take the fight to them. We need to take them out before they get to us," Matteo said.

"We put surveillance on all their top guys and get ahead of it," Giovanni said.

"Let's get everything set up for the security part of this. You guys move in here with your women. Then tomorrow, we start taking out Volkov's men," I said. "Any more ideas? Let me know. I need to check on Annika. Everyone, stay safe."

I headed up to our room to check on Annika. She was sitting up in bed. She smiled when I walked in.

"How are you feeling?" I asked.

"Better. I wish I could take a bath. I'm ready for these stitches to be out," she said.

"You have about a week or so. But I can run you a bath. Just keep your arms out on the sides of the tub," I said.

"How am I supposed to wash myself?"

I wiggled my eyebrows at her, and she laughed.

"Oh," she said with a smile.

I ran her a bath and came in. She was sitting up with her feet on the floor. I pulled her nightgown over her head, and she was so sore we did not bother the putting panties on last night. I picked her up and set her in the warm water.

"Oh god, this feels so amazing."

I washed her hair first and moved down her body. I washed everything as I went. I washed in between her legs, and she closed her eyes.

"I'm sorry, Bella. I'll be quick," I said, not wanting to get her aroused while she was in so much pain and banged up.

I picked her up out of the tub and set her on a bench. I dried her off and put her in a fluffy robe.

"You want to go back to bed?"

"No. Can you put me on the lounge on the terrace? I want some sun."

I put her on the terrace and grabbed the book she was reading by the bed. Vera brought up lunch, and we sat outside, enjoying the day.

"We are making a move on your father starting tomorrow. We're moving in our cousins with their women for safety," I told her.

"I would like to have people here. This house is so big. It would be awesome to have family dinners."

"We think my mother might have been in on the assault, Annika." I looked at her.

"I'm not a bit surprised if she is part of it."

"If she is, she signed her death warrant, and she will no longer be part of this family. They also went to your father, and we're presuming your father knows everything Salvatore knows."

"Taking down her own children for power. Our parents are one and the same," Annika said.

"Ivan has two brothers, Igor and Andre. They are part of the family. They own a boxing ring on the south side. There are brutal, raping and torturing women. They need to be removed as well as Ivan. My father has no brothers to step in. I would take them out first," Annika said to me. I smiled at her.

"You were born to be a leader. Your father underestimated you. I'll contact the guys, and we will rid the world of them. First, we spend the day together."

Grazia came up and sat next to her mom. She had been very worried.

"Baby girl, I have a surprise to tell you," Annika said to her daughter.

"What is it?" she said with excitement.

"You're going have a baby sister or brother."

"I am? I'm going to be a big sister?" She jumped up and ran out of the room, screaming to tell the world. We both laughed out loud.

"Well, I guess she's happy about it," I said, laughing.

The next morning, everyone met in the office at 4:00 a.m. We needed to hit the Russians early and hard. We brought in Drifter, the MC sniper, to help.

"Good morning, everyone. Today is a good day for war. I say all security measures have been implemented. The weapons have been moved with the Greeks' help. We take this war to their doorstep and keep it off ours. We have undercover men in their territory placed all over their turf. We will take out as many of their men as possible, starting today. I want heavy surveillance on Volkov, Salvatore, and my mother. She is still in the house. I want Volkov and Salvatore taken alive if possible. Drifter is already on the roof across the gym. We take out the brothers today," I said.

Everyone suited up in armor and loaded up. We were headed out in fifteen minutes. We had vehicles out front. We pulled up in a junkie car with tinted windows. We fit right in the neighborhood.

"We are here," I said into the mic.

"Ivan has not shown up yet. The other two brothers are inside. No one else is there. Cameras are in our favor," Luca said, watching everything. "Both men are working out. They are not armed," Luca said.

"I want Igor taken alive. Kill Andrei. Keep us posted when you know Ivan is close, Luca. Let's move," I said.

"Ten-four," Luca said.

Giovanni, Matteo, and Dante headed to the gym. The rest stayed in the cars and kept guard. Drifter was on the roof to take anyone out who was a problem. We entered the building quietly. The gym was small. It didn't even have a boxing ring. I signaled everyone to move about.

"Andrei is lifting weights, and Igor is using a punching bag," Luca said.

I shot Igor in the knee at the same time Giovanni shot Andrei in the head. The weights Andrei was holding hits him in the chest.

Igor screamed in pain for his brother. I would have felt bad, except I knew what they had done to all those women they tortured.

"Secure him," I told Matteo and Dante.

They zip tied him and gagged him and searched for weapons. "Take him out and throw him in the trunk of the car."

"Team 1 takes him to the basement." I sent Giovanni with him. I got in the other car with team 2.

"Brothers are secured," I said to Luca.

"Ten-four. Ivan is headed your way. ETA is fifteen minutes," Luca said.

"Drifter, as soon as he is inside the building, take him out," I said.

"Ten-four," Drifter said.

Ivan pulled his car to the curb and walked in the building. Drifter shot once. The only thing we could hear was the glass breaking. Ivan dropped to the floor.

"Let's go," I said. We all went back in the building and burned it to the ground. We headed back to the house and regrouped.

A few hours later, Luca came into my office.

"Fourteen of Volkov's men have been taken out already this morning," Luca said as he walked in.

"He's also absolutely broke. We have taken everything financially from him. And listen to this. He put everything in his daughter's name. He was using her as the fall guy if the government got involved. She owns property all over the city. He just forges her name to everything," Luca said.

"How much property are we talking about?" I said.

"Two casinos, four strip clubs, apartment buildings on Lake Michigan, six restaurants, and a shit ton more of smaller buildings and a warehouse with four hotels. We took close to $800 million from him," Luca said.

"He can take those and turn them into cash fast if he's forging her name," Giovanni said.

"Will she sign them over to you, Angelino?" Matteo asked.

"Get the paperwork ready on all the properties and get our lawyer involved. I want it done today. I'll talk to her, but she wants me to handle everything," I said.

"We're going to own most of the city after today," Giovanni said.

"Yes, we are," Santos said.

"Look into all the properties and see if they are legit or if they are profitable. Let's make the best out of this," I said.

"If anyone has any suggestions for some of the properties, let us know. We are family, and we grow as a family," Giovanni said.

The cousins looked at each other, realizing the faith that me and Giovanni had in them.

"We have a few ideas we would discuss after the business with Volkov is done," Dante said.

"Luca, keep us posted on how many men fall and when you locate Salvatore," I said.

"I will."

I walked up to check on Annika. She was standing in the back bathroom, brushing her teeth. She had already dressed in a yellow sundress that came to her knees. Her hair was in a bun. She turned when she saw me.

"Good morning," I said, kissing her lips.

"Good morning. You're up? Are you feeling better?"

"I do. I'm still sore, but I need to move around a little. Grazia worries when I'm in bed. I need her to know I'm going to be okay."

Her face is still black and blue. She tried to cover it up with makeup.

"I can carry you down for breakfast and then maybe sit you in a lounge by the pool. You'll still be relaxing, but you'll look like you feel better," I said.

"Yes, please." I reached down and put her sandals on her feet. I picked her up and carried her down the stairs for breakfast.

"I can't wait till I'm better. You and the jeans and white T-shirt are killing me," she said, making me laugh.

"I might break you when I finally get to touch you," I said. Then she laughed.

We ate breakfast, and I helped her walk outside to a lounger. Mia took Grazia swimming.

"I've got business to attend to in the basement. Your plan worked perfectly."

"When did you take them?"

"Early this morning. Here's your phone. When you are ready, call me. I'll come get you and carry you where you want to go. Vera will be here to check on you shortly."

"I love you," she said.

"I love you." I kissed her on the lips and headed to the basement.

I texted, "I am headed to the basement to speak to our guest."

Dante replied, "I am heading that way."

We both got to the dungeon, and it was an actual dungeon, with cells lining both walls. There were still brackets on the walls to chain prisoners to. Igor was secured to the wall with his arms spread out beside him.

"Good morning, sunshine," Dante said to him.

"What the fuck do you want? You're not getting shit out of me. Ivan is going to fucking kill you," he spit out rage. Dante laughed a sadistic laugh.

I let him handle the interrogation. It was what he was great at.

"Oh, Igor, come on now. You're not being very nice," Dante said, messing with him.

"Fuck you," he spat.

"Tsk, tsk. Such a nasty temper," Dante said. Dante grabbed the shears and walked over to him. "This can be easy or hard, Igor. Where is Salvatore?"

"No clue. I don't fuck with you Italians."

He started screaming as he cut off a pinky.

"Wrong answer. Where is he? I won't ask a second time."

"I don't fucking know."

He screamed as Dante removed his other pinky.

"So stubborn. This is going to be a long day if you keep this up," Dante said in a childlike demeanor, taunting Igor.

"One last time and I start removing teeth," Dante said.

Igor looked up at Dante. "Fine. I fucking hate the Italians. He is in an apartment building on the lake. The penthouse, Lakeview," he said.

I texted Luca the information to verify and see if he could locate them.

"See, that was not so hard, was it?" he taunted him. "Enjoy the rest of your day. We have more questions, and we'll be back for a chat," Dante said and washed and headed upstairs.

"Hello," I said, answering the phone.

Luca said, "I checked the camera's footage. Salvatore is in the building."

"Perfect. I'll have him picked up," I said.

I texted, "I need everyone in my office in 5 minutes."

I headed to my office and met everyone there.

"We have a location on Salvatore, thanks to Dante's skills," I said.

I explained where he was.

"We need a plan. The building has light security, a guard in the front foyer. The penthouse does have a key code for entry. Salvatore never leaves the building. He goes down twice a day to the gym," Luca said.

"We need people who are not obvious," I said. "The bikers and all our people will be seen a mile away. Giovanni, what about getting a few of the Greeks here?" I asked.

"He said he will help any way he can. I'll call him now."

"We get the Greeks inside, and they secure Salvatore, and we bring them back here." Giovanni walked back into the office.

"Argyros is sending six men to help until we have Volkov. They'll be here in a few hours," Giovanni said.

"When we bring them back here, I want Salvatore to myself. Let's get set for anything. As soon as they land, we will head that way," I said.

"We have all the paperwork ready for Annika to sign. The lawyer will be here shortly with all the titles," Luca said.

"I'll go talk to her now."

I headed out to the terrace, where she had her eyes closed.

"Hey, Bella, let me take you upstairs for a bit. You need to rest," I said, picking her up and taking her upstairs. I put her in the bed.

I put some pj's on her and tucked her in.

"I need to ask you something."

"Ask away."

"We found out your father put all his property, legal and illegal, in your name. That way, if the feds ever found out anything illegal, you would take the fall for it. I need you to sign them over to me because he has been forging your name."

"Okay," she said.

"Okay? That's it?"

"Of course. You're the best thing in my life. I trust you."

"I love you. I'll keep you in the loop about the businesses, and then when they are legal and Volkov is dead, I'll sign them back over. Get some rest. I'll be back up in a little bit for you to sign the papers. I love you." I kissed her on the lips and forehead and then left her to rest.

The Greeks landed a few hours later, and they headed straight to the penthouse and waited for Salvatore to head to the gym. One guy went in and acted like he was working out. Luca called me and told me all the properties were in my name and it was filed. I had him check for anything else in her name. I stayed home with Annika while they secured the penthouse.

Luca texted, "Fourteen more guys have been taken care of. Cops think it's a gang war."

I replied, "Good."

I walked down to the dungeon, and they had Salvatore secured to the wall in his cell.

"Mr. Rossi, I'm Leander, head of our security team and Argyros's son. And these are my misfits." He introduced all of them. Leander was just announced as his son. He had been hiding him all his life.

"We appreciate your help," I said, shaking his hand.

"We have rooms prepared for all of you. Any of you good at getting information out of people?" I asked.

"Orion is," Leander said.

"Even women?' I asked.

"If they are deserving, I don't have an issue," Orion said.

"Well, I'm not sure we're going to have to use you yet, depending if the woman we think betrayed us is involved or not."

All the men went upstairs, leaving me, Giovanni, and Orion.

"Well, Salvatore welcome home," Giovanni said.

"What's the matter, Salvatore? Cat got your tongue?" I said to him tauntingly.

"It's okay. You don't have to speak right now. We're going to leave you overnight to think about things and the torture that is ahead of you. Have a good night," Giovanni told him, laughing.

Orion headed to his room, and Giovanni and I headed to my office for a drink. Luca walked in.

"I have an idea for one of our new properties," he said.

"Go ahead," Giovanni said.

"My brothers and I have been speaking. We think with my cyber skills and Rocco in security, we should open a security company, a security division. A cyber side and a bodyguard side. Matteo, Santos, and Dante can train in defense. Matteo and Santos can handle the business part. Then we hire people to take over training and run it. We'll bring in more cyber techs. It'll be another legitimate business," Luca said.

"I like it," I said.

"I do too. What site are you looking at?" Giovanni asked.

"There's an office building downtown. We are not sure what it was used for. There are no businesses in the building," Luca said.

"Okay. Take some guys with you and hire a designer so it's planned out properly. Whatever you and your brothers decide on the design, we're going to let you guys handle this project," I said.

"Anything else?" Giovanni asked.

"We would each like to have a penthouse on the lake properties, if that's possible," Luca said.

"Absolutely, it is. Pick what you want and make sure top-level security is added to the buildings. You're a head at the table. This belongs to all of us."

"I say to also let our men use the building, our security people who you hire for the new security company. They can use the lower levels of the building apartments," I said.

"Thank you," he said.

"Damn, we are going more legitimate every day," Giovanni said, looking at me.

"Legit with a murderous side," I said, laughing. Giovanni started laughing as well.

"So have you spoken to Amelia yet?" I asked.

Over the next month, Annika healed. I still had Salvatore in the basement. I had been torturing him for two weeks. I wanted Annika to see him like this, like he left her, if she decided she wanted to.

"Hey, Bella, you look amazing," I said, walking into the library. She was wearing flowy light pink maxi skirt and a white V-neck shirt with sandals. Her hair flowed around her.

"Hey there, sexy," she said. She stood up to kiss me.

"You know we found Salvatore," I said.

"Yes. Is he dead?"

"Not yet. I didn't know if you wanted to show him you survived or not. He's been punished every day."

"I would love to face him," she said. We made our way down to the basement.

"This is an actual dungeon," she said. The old fire sconce from centuries ago was still on the walls.

"I'm warning you. There will be blood everywhere, and he's not in great shape," I said to her to prepare her. She nodded.

We got to his cell, and he raised his head slowly. He was missing several fingers, missing teeth, had broken nose, and had burns and cuts everywhere.

"Look at you," she said. "Not looking so tough now."

She passed back and forth in front of him.

"Well, you failed, just like my father did. I'm not dead or broken. But both of you will meet your fate soon enough."

He did his best to spit at her without a tongue and no spit from being dehydrated. She laughed.

"Is that all you've got? What, cat got your tongue?" she asked him, and I laughed because I asked him that two weeks ago.

He was still pissed. She picked up a knife from the table, and I looked at her.

"Bella?" I said her name as a question.

"I'm good," she said. I nodded at her.

She stepped in front of him and put the knife under his chin. Salvatore pissed on himself.

"This dress is new. Don't mess it up," she said. She looked vicious. "Your life is in my hands. How does it feel?" He blinked really fast. "That's what I thought. You're brave beating on women a fourth your size. You tried to end my life and take my child I'm carrying." He just stared her in the eye, shaking.

Then she sliced his throat. She started at his left ear and came across his throat all the way to the right, blood spraying everywhere. I walked up behind her. She watched his life drain from him.

"I really liked this dress," I said.

She turned around. "Yeah, I'm a bit of a mess."

"Strip. There is a shower over there. Leave your clothes here and I'll join you in a second."

She headed to the shower. I removed the body and threw him in the incinerator, right along with both of our clothes. I sent a text for one of the guys to clean up. I stepped in the shower with Annika.

"Are you okay?" I asked.

"I am. Maybe I'm a little twisted. I'm not even fazed," she said.

"You're not twisted. We've just been through way too much. You're perfect."

I kissed her softly, and it turned animalistic fast. She reached down and fisted my cock, making me moan. I reached between us and rubbed her clit.

"Finger me, please, Angelino," she begged.

I stuck two fingers in her tight pussy and fingered her hard. She raised her leg so I could get better access. She continued to stroke my cock.

"Oh, you're so wet. Fuck." She loved when I talked dirty.

"Yes," she said.

"You like my fingers in your pussy? How would you like them in your ass? Maybe my big cock in your pussy and the toy in your ass. Is that what you want?"

"Oh…Angelino. I'm going to come!" She screamed my name as I finger fucked her hard.

I turned her around and bent her over, her ass sticking out. I slipped my cock through her lips.

"Ah, you're so tight. I love your pussy surrounding my cock."

"Fuck me harder, Angel."

"I don't want to hurt the baby."

"You won't. I need it hard, please."

I grabbed her hips and started slamming into her. Damn, she felt good. She reached down and played with her clit.

"That's my girl. Play with your pussy and come all over my dick."

And with that, she clamped around me with a scream. I was slamming into her and felt my own orgasm take over.

"Fuck!" I bellowed out.

We both stood there, breathless. I kissed her on her back.

"I love you."

"I love you too," she said.

We finished showering and headed upstairs.

"Dr. Merida is coming over to do a sonogram to check everything and see if he can tell the sex of the baby," she said.

"Good. We can pick colors for the nursery," I said.

We planned on having an area set up for the baby in our room until the baby got older. We headed down to the clinic, and they were ready. Everything was already set up.

Annika sat on the table in sweats and a T-shirt she put on in the dungeon.

"Let's see if we can find out the sex of the baby," the doc said, moving the wand around. "There's your baby. Looks like the baby is sucking its thumb." We both laughed. "Looks like you're having a boy," he said.

I squeezed her hand. I was so happy. "We need to celebrate tonight," I said.

"What do you have in mind?" she asked.

"I say we get the chef to make our favorites and have a family get-together. Leander and his team can join us. Maybe we'll have out it outside on the terrace. Play some music and have some dancing."

"That sounds like a perfect evening," Annika said.

Angelino

"Angel, is Amelia safe?"

"Yes, Bella. The shop owner killed the guy to protect Amelia. They are on their way back now. They want to get married today so Draco does not try to kidnap Amelia again."

"Thank God. I will get everything together. Can you call everyone, including her family?"

We had the ceremony at 5:00 p.m., and Annika outdid herself. You could not tell it was planned in a few hours. My brother never looked happier. Amelia was an amazing part of this family. We spent the evening drinking and laughing.

Annika

Three weeks later, Giovanni and Angel left the house to take care of some business. I was working on my next decorating project, which was Giovanni's office or the main office of the house. The room was huge. I wanted it to reflect the past, the present, and the future and make it comfortable for the many cousins. The Rossis didn't hide their women from their business. They embraced them. I was thinking of a smaller version of the dining table but ebony wood, with comfortable armchairs and pictures of the family and the castle.

I was looking through pictures of them and heard Grazia scream. One of the guards was ahead of me, and he busted down her door and stood in the doorframe.

"Put her down now," the guard said.

"No, she is coming with me," the guy said. How did he get in here?

"You need to let her go," Malone said calmly.

"No, you're going to die, and she is coming with me," he said.

Grazia was struggling and crying. I couldn't see her, but I could hear her. I ran to our room a door down and pulled Angelino's pistol from our nightstand. I checked the clip and chamber and took it off safety and headed back. I stayed outside the room. My guard pulled his gun out. The guy shot him, and he dropped.

"What a damn idiot," the guy said as Grazia screamed. She was terrified.

"Shut up, you little bitch. We're leaving. I'm taking you to your new home."

Our second guard, Tommy, stepped in and stood next to the door.

"Jacobs, you need to let her go. She is innocent."

"No. We are walking out of here or she dies," Jacobs threatened.

Think…think. The only way out was through the door. They couldn't go out the balcony. It was too far of a drop. *The balcony!* I ran back to our room with the gun in my hand and walked out to the balcony. I jumped the divider between our balcony's and Grazia's. It was about a foot. Thank God for skinny jeans and heels instead of a skirt. I kept the heels on just in case I needed to kick the hell out of someone. I quietly stepped to the glass doors and stood in the corner. Jacobs, one of our guards, had an arm around Grazia and the gun pointed in front of him at Tommy. I didn't open the door. I aimed and pulled the trigger, shattering the glass. Jacobs dropped dead. I walked through the shattered door across the glass and flipped the gun on safety and handed it to the guard. I picked up Grazia. The guard looked impressed.

"It's okay, honey. Mommy's here. He can't hurt you. Mommy took care of it.

"Call the men, please, and get rid of him. And get Malone taken care of," I told Tommy.

I walked out of the door with Grazia. She was shaking but not hurt. She was sobbing on my chest.

"It's okay, honey. Daddy will be home soon."

I called the doctor and had him come over to give her something to calm her down. He was only a few minutes away. He checked her out and then gave her something to rest. I held her tight and left her on my chest as I watched the fire in the room and waited for Angelino.

Both Angelino and Giovanni ran and stopped and looked at me. Angelino came over and wrapped his arms around both of us.

"I cleaned her up and gave her something to rest," I told them to reassure them. Giovanni came over in front of me.

"Can I hold her?" he said, looking shattered. I handed her over, and Angelino walked up and embraced me like his life depended on it.

"I couldn't breathe when Tommy told me someone tried to take Grazia. You killed him?" he asked, surprised.

"I did." He didn't say anything else. "We need to put Grazia in another room, the one on the other side or across the hall. I don't want her in that room anymore."

"I'll get someone to move her things and replace what needs to be replaced," Angelino said. Giovanni sat on the couch, holding his niece. They both started to calm down after holding her and knowing she was okay.

"Any idea who he was working for?" Angelino asked Giovanni.

"No, but we need to find out."

I called Luca as the guys fussed over Grazia.

"Yes, boss," he said to me when he answered the call.

"Luca, we had an inside breach today. I need Jacobs's calls traced and see who he has been contacting. I also need you to check everyone else's calls. I need to know if we have anyone else that's a traitor."

"Yes, ma'am."

"Also, we need two highly trained guards on Grazia. She goes nowhere without them."

"I'm on it. Anything else?"

"How is Malone?"

"He's going to make it."

"Thank God. Thank you." I ended the call and turned around. Both guys were staring at me. Maybe I just stepped over a line. But I didn't care. For Grazia, they could punish me.

"Brother?" Giovanni said to Angelino.

"I know," he said as they stared at me. Were they speaking in their own language or what?

"I'm going to take Grazia to see Amelia if that's okay. She is worried. Gracie's been wanting to learn how to sew. Maybe she can show her to keep her mind off things."

Angelino looked up at me to make sure I was going to be good with her letting her go. I nodded.

Angelino and I walked to Grazia's room. There was blood and glass everywhere. He had not said much to me. I was not sure what he was thinking. He walked around the room and looked around. He stopped in the middle of the room and looked up at me.

"I don't have words, Bella."

"It's okay. There is no need."

"Yes, there is a need. I don't know how to thank you. Words are nothing. You saved our daughter and not once thought of yourself. You took him out when two guards couldn't."

"They would have both given their lives, Angelino. They're loyal."

"Yes, they are, but they are not as smart as you are. I owe you more than I have to give for what you have done for Grazia. You protected her with your life." He turned his eyes to the floor, and when he looked up, there were tears in his eyes. I walked up to him and wrapped my arms around him.

"She's okay. We will always make sure she is."

"I don't know what I would have done if they got her."

Trying to make light of the situation and to calm Angelino down, I said, "Come on. You know I'm psycho. They would have never gotten past me." He looked at me with a small smile.

"You're a fucking badass, and that doesn't even cover it."

"I need a drink," I told him, and he laughed.

"I can help you with that. Maybe a Shirley temple," he said, making me laugh. We headed to our room.

Angelino

"What? What do you mean someone tried to kidnap Grazia?"

My brother stiffened beside me, and I put the guard on speaker.

"Jacobs had her at gunpoint and was trying to leave with her. Jacobs shot Malone when he tried to protect her," Tommy said.

"You stopped Jacobs? Where is he now?"

"He's dead, sir," Tommy said.

"Good job, Tommy," I said.

"Sir, I didn't kill him. Your wife did."

"I'm driving back to the house." Giovanni and I looked at each other. "What happened? Is Grazia okay?"

"She is fine, sir. She is with your wife. Your wife came up behind him on the balcony and shot him in the head, killing him," Tommy said.

I didn't even know she knew how to use a gun.

"We are on our way back. Get the body taken care of."

"We already did, sir. Your wife gave that order." I hung up.

"Who the hell did you marry? GI Jane?" Giovanni looked at me as he said it seriously.

"I have no clue. She keeps surprising the hell out of me. Let's get home to them. This job can wait."

My mind was racing, thinking of what happened. We got home, and the guard told us where they were. We headed to our room, and Annika was sitting on the couch with a sleeping Grazia on her chest. I walked over and wrapped my arms around them both.

"I cleaned her up and gave her something to rest," Annika said.

"Can I hold her?" Giovanni asked.

I walked up and embraced Annika for being so brave.

"I could not breathe when Tommy told me someone tried to take Grazia. You killed him?" I asked her, surprised she did.

"I did," she said with no emotion at all. "We need to put Grazia in another room, the one on the other side or across the hall. I don't want her in that room anymore," she said, thinking of our daughter.

"I'll get someone to move her things and replace what needs to be replaced," I said.

"Any idea who he was working for?" I asked Giovanni.

"No, but we need to find out," Annika said, picking up her phone. I looked at Giovanni, and we were both wondering what she was doing. She put the phone on speaker.

"Yes, boss," Luca said when he answered the call. It was the same thing our cousins said when Giovanni or I called. They respected her and saw her as their boss.

"Luca, we had an inside breach today. I need Jacobs's calls traced and see who he has been contacting. I also need you to check everyone else's calls. I need to know if we have anyone else that's a traitor."

"Yes, ma'am."

"Also, we always need two highly trained guards on Grazia. She goes nowhere without them."

"I'm on it. Anything else?"

"Malone, is he okay?"

She was checking on our guards, making sure they were safe. She was meant to be my wife.

"He's going make it," Luca said.

"Thank God. Thank you." She ended the call and turned to us.

"Brother?" Giovanni said, knowing he saw what I saw. Annika stepped into a head role with ease.

"I know," I said as we both stared at her. We agreed about what Annika represented from just watching her.

Giovanni took Grazia to visit Amelia, giving me space to talk to my wife.

Annika and I walked to Grazia's room. There was blood and glass everywhere. I walked around the room, looked, and stopped in the middle.

"I don't have words, Bella."

"It's okay. There is no need."

"Yes, there is a need. I don't know how to thank you. Words are nothing. You saved our daughter and not once thought of yourself. You took him out when two guards couldn't."

"They would have both given their lives, Angelino. They're loyal."

"Yes, they are, but they are not as smart as you are. I owe you more than I could ever give for what you have done for Grazia. You protected her with your life." I looked at the floor. The emotions were burning my eyes.

Annika put her arms around me. "She's okay. We will always make sure she is."

"I don't know what I would have done if they got her."

"Come on. You know I'm psycho. They would have never gotten past me," she said, making me smile.

"You're a fucking badass, and that doesn't even cover it." We headed back to our room.

"Do you want to talk about what happened?"

"I did what I had to do to protect our daughter. Jacobs had her trapped in the room. All I know was I had to get to her."

"Where did you learn to shoot a gun?"

"Boris, the guard my father killed. My mother had an affair with him. But Boris loved me and treated me like I was his own. He took us to the gun range often. He always said a lady should know how to protect herself. I always thought he showed me how so I could protect myself against my father."

"You have a hell of an aim. Remind me to stay on your good side," I told her, and we both laughed.

"Annika, I've been around several heads of the Mafia men in my day, but you're the first to ever surprise me," I said, letting my words sink in.

"I'm no leader. I was protecting our daughter. I would give my life for you both."

"I know you will. I know it in my soul. You protected our daughter better than a bodyguard ever could. I am more than impressed with you. I mean all of you. I want to ask you something, and you are allowed to say no."

"What is it?"

"You are my wife and partner. We are equals in this family. We'll want everyone to know you hold a seat in our family if you'll accept it. I want you part of the business on a day-to-day operation when you're not working. And if you accept this, I want to throw a party for all the families on neutral ground. Families from other cities will come in, and we will announce your seat. That way, they know you're not my weakness but my greatest asset."

She had tears running down her face. "Are you serious? You think I'm worthy of that?"

"You didn't think twice about yourself today. You killed a man and picked up our daughter to take care of her. Then you ordered our men around like you've been doing it since birth. They all respect you like you are their queen already. I think this is the next step in making our family stronger. What do you say?"

"I say yes," she said, running and jumping in my arms.

"Thank you so much for believing in me. I won't ever let you down."

"You couldn't let me down even if you tried. Can I tell you how turned on I am knowing you dropped a guy dead with one shot and walked around owning this place?" She laughed.

"You're a little twisted, you know that?"

"Yes, and you are too," I said to her as she backed up a couple of steps and pulled her shirt over her head.

Her beautiful breast poked out of her red bra.

"Damn, Bella, this might not last long." She laughed. I stalked over to her and pulled my shirt over my head. She grabbed my pants as I did hers. Both of us were in a rush to get each other's clothes off. We both pulled off her pants and left them in a heap.

"Matching panties?" I said, eyeing her. She reached to pull her red thong off.

"Leave them on." She did as I asked. I kiss her roughly as I backed her against the small dining table. I picked her up and sat her on the table. She stroked my cock.

"That feels so good," I said to her with a moan. I flicked my finger under her bra and played with her nipple. She removed her hand from my cock and slid her panties aside to touch her pussy.

"Grrrrr…fuck, Bella, yes, play with your pussy." She rolled her head back and started moaning. I pulled her panties and slid my dick inside her. I grabbed her hips and slammed into her hard.

"Does this cock feel good?"

"Feels so good. I'm…I'm going to come!" she screamed her release. Her wet pussy clenched around my cock, making it hard to keep it together. I picked her up and took her to the bed.

"On all fours." She turned around. "You're so fucking sexy," I told her, staring at her ass.

I ran my finger up her clit, and she moaned. I stuck my fingers in her wet pussy, moving them slowly in and out. She was meeting my strokes, backing into my fingers. I pulled her panties hard, ripping them off. I reached up and removed her bra. I put my fingers back inside, and with my other hand, I played with her nipple.

"More, more, Angelino," she whimpered.

I took my hand off her nipple and circled her asshole, and she clenched.

"Relax, babe. Relax. Do you want me to stop?"

"No" was all she said.

I reached around and rubbed her clit. I removed my fingers from her pussy, and she inserted one finger in her ass, slowly moving it in and out.

"Angelino," she said, panting.

"You need me to stop?"

"Please, don't stop."

"What do you want, Bella? Tell me?"

"I don't know. It feels really good." I worked her faster, and she was panting.

"Play with your pussy." She started rubbing her clit. I stuck two fingers in her pussy as I fingered her ass with the other hand slowly.

"Angel, I need your dick, please."

"Where do you want my dick?"

"Everywhere, please," she said, moaning.

I pulled the little lube out of the drawer and lathered up my dick.

"Keep playing with your pussy. I'm going to play in your ass."

I stuck the tip to her hole, and she laid her head on the bed with her ass in the air.

"God, woman, you're so fucking hot." I stuck the tip in and worked it in and out slowly so she got used to me.

"You like my big dick in your ass?"

"Yes. Faster, harder, make me come." I started pumping in her ass over and over.

"Your tight ass is going to make me come."

"Aahhh. Angel!" she screamed she came hard, driving me over the edge. I came inside her beautiful ass.

"You're so amazing. I can never get enough of you," I said as I pulled out. I leaned her up so she was flush against me and kissed her neck.

I picked her up and carried her to the bathroom. I ran us a hot bath and stepped inside with her in my arms. She was laying against my chest.

"I tried to tell you how stunning you are, but words are not enough. You've always been beautiful, but now that you've put on weight and you're pregnant with my child, you just get sexier by the day."

"I think you're the sexy one with all the sexy tattoos and ripped muscles."

I laughed. "Well, I can get you all tattooed up so you match me," I told her jokingly.

"You would allow me to get tattoos?" I was just joking with her, never thinking in a million years she would want a tattoo.

"Hell yes! Keep talking like that and I'm going to take you again right here in this bathtub." She laughed out loud.

"You wouldn't think it was ugly or trashy?"

"No way. It's sexy as hell as long as it's done right. What are you thinking?" She stayed quiet. "You can tell me."

"I want a sleeve on my left arm. I want you and Grazia and the Rossi name. Something sexy and fierce. I want it from my shoulder all the way down to my fingertips.

"Holy shit, really? I'm going to come thinking about that. We have a guy. I can have him come over here and work with you on your design."

"Yes. I would love that, please."

This woman with a sleeve. Fuck, no Mafia man will fuck with her. They are going to fear her before it's over, I thought to myself.

"You ready to go out?"

"Yes. Can we go get Grazia and see if your brother and Amelia want to do a movie night or something in the theater? And then can she sleep with us tonight." This woman kept chiseling away a little bit of my heart each day.

"Of course. You never have to ask."

We lay out on the sofa, and I placed my hand on her stomach, and I felt our son move.

"Omg, did you feel that?" she asked. I laughed.

"Yes. He must love me," I said, and we both laughed.

So that's how we spent our evening in the theater, watching movies with the family. Grazia slept between us. The next day, I called Max, our tattoo artist, and he got started on Annika's sleeve.

A couple of days passed, and Giovanni had been distant. Amelia left him.

"So have you spoken to Amelia yet?" I asked.

"Yes. She wants the divorce. I'm flying to her father's after I leave here. I'm such an idiot. How could I have not treated her better? She deserves better than me. I have so many anger and trust issues. I was so scared of the things Annika has been through, and I didn't want to feel that if Amelia went through it."

"Go get her back."

My brother pushed Amelia away to protect himself, and she left and went back to her father.

Giovanni came back some time in the night empty-handed. He had been in his room for days and wouldn't come out. I called Amelia myself and explained why Giovanni was the way he was. How he got the blunt of our mother's abuse when we were out with our father learning the business. Amelia was crying after I told her a few stories. She flew back tonight, and Giovanni texted to thank me and told me she was about three months pregnant. She and Annika would give birth about the same time.

Annika

Things with Angelino's mother continued to be the same. She still tried to act like she ran the house when the brothers were not around.

"Hello, Tommy. How can I help you?" I answered the phone. I left him with Grazia as one of her bodyguards.

"Ma'am, we have an issue with your mother-in-law. She's been really ugly to Grazia and kicked us out of the room. I will break the door down if needed, but I figured it would be better if you handled it."

"I'm on my way."

It took me all of two seconds to get to the room, and when I entered, Sophia was shaking my daughter.

"You're so stupid. How do you not know how to read even a little?" She smacked her on the side of her leg, and I flew to her as fast as I could. I shoved Sophia off her and picked up my daughter. Tommy came up behind me, and I handed Grazia to him.

"Go with Tommy, honey. Mommy needs to deal with this nasty lady."

"Take Grazia out in the hall for me, please. And call Angelino and let him know what's going on," I said to Tommy. He left Malone, the other bodyguard, in the room with me.

Then I turned to Sophia. "What the fuck do you think you're doing? You dare to lay a finger on my daughter? You're either brave or very stupid."

"Mind your own damn business. She's my granddaughter. I'm allowed to punish her!" she bellowed. "She is stupid like her mother."

And no sooner did those words get out of her mouth than I came across her face with an elbow to her nose, knocking her over the dollhouse and shattering her nose.

"You will never come near my daughter again. This I promise you. I will kill you myself if I hear you have," I said through gritted teeth. "Find out where Angelino is and escort her to him, please. Do not let her out of your sight." She was pissed because they were listening to me.

"Yes, ma'am."

I walked out the door and took my daughter from Tommy and headed down to the kitchen.

"I'm sorry, baby girl. The bad lady will never talk to you again."

She cried on my shoulder as I took her downstairs. I sat her on the counter when I got to the kitchen.

"You're so smart, baby girl. Don't listen to the mean lady."

"But I can't read. I have trouble."

"Well, honey, you're still very little. I will help you. You know Mommy had trouble reading all through school. But now I'm a doctor. I had to learn my own way to read. Your father and I are here always."

I looked at the pink and red marks on her arms from being shaken. And there was a handprint on her leg. *I should have killed her*, I thought to myself. Giovanni and Angelino walked in with their mother. I broke her nose. She had blood all over her face and all over her shirt. Giovanni and Angelino smiled at me. Grazia clung to me as she sat on the counter. Their mother had a smile on her face, like she stole a cookie.

"So Mother says you elbowed her in the face," Giovanni said with a smile on his face.

They both knew her well enough to know she deserved it. They just wanted to know what the story was.

"I did." That was all I said.

"See, I told you. Now get her away from my granddaughter and out of the house!" she bellowed.

"No!" Grazia screamed, holding me tighter. I embraced her.

"I'm not going anywhere, baby girl. But she is."

"What happened?" Angelino asked. He knew me well enough to know I was pissed.

"I told you what happened. I was playing with Grazia, and your wife didn't like it and punched me and threatened to kill me. Isn't that right, Grazia?" She looked at her with slits for eyes, trying to scare Grazia into lying for her.

"You do not speak to my daughter ever. I told you that already. Or you can join your friend and have no tongue," I said to her.

"See? She's just trying to get rid of me and trying to get me out of the house," she told the guys.

"I'm not trying to do anything. You're headed to the basement right now. You are nothing but a tyrant and a bully."

Giovanni started laughing out loud. "I love your wife," he said to Angelino. Tommy and Malone walked in the kitchen. They were standing outside the door.

"Tommy, Malone, please escort Sophia down to the dungeon. We have a spot that's been waiting for her," I said to the guards. They both took her arm and escorted her in the other direction.

"Are you going to stand there and let her speak to me that way and treat me this way?" she spoke.

"You better be glad I'm allowing you to continue breathing after hurting my daughter. You just better hope that all the rumors that are going around about you are not true. You know, the ones about the Russians," Angelino said to her.

"Yes, Mother, we have a friend, Orion, who has been dying to meet you," Giovanni said to her. Orion was the one who was going to interrogate her or torture her for information.

Angelino came over and put his hand on Grazia. "Are you okay?" he asked her.

"Grandma said I was stupid. She shook me and slapped me. See?" she said, showing her daddy her marks. They were both pissed.

Giovanni walked up to the other side of Grazia.

"She's gone. Uncle Gio won't let anyone touch you again," he said to her. Grazia put her arms around Giovanni. He pulled her to his chest.

"Thank you for saving me, Mommy," she said to me.

"I will always save you," I said to her.

"How about we go swimming and forget about the stupid lady?" Giovanni said to his niece.

"Yes, please." And they left.

"Wow, I've created a monster," Angelino said to me, making me laugh.

"How is that?"

"My sweet broken wife has turned into a fierce and protective queen," he said, impressed.

"I snapped when I saw her hurting her and she called her stupid. I could have killed her myself."

"I've never seen anyone talk to my mother like that except you and Amelia. Everyone has always feared her," he said.

"She is nothing but a power-hungry bully. I was raised by one of those. I let all her crap go over the last month or so. But I won't bow down to Grazia being hurt. She is mine to protect."

He grabbed me by the back of my head and kissed me like he might lose me.

"I'm so proud of you more every day, I can't even tell you how much.

"Thank you, Angelino."

"I want you now," Angelino said to me with a hunger in his eyes I had never seen before.

I put my arms around his neck, and he grabbed my legs and wrapped my legs around his waist. He headed to his office because it was closer. He locked the door and stalked toward me. He dropped to his knees and reached under my dress and pulled my panties off.

"Put your foot on the sofa," he said. I did as he said, and it left me spread wide. He lifted my dress up, and I grabbed it. He licked me from asshole to clit.

"God, you taste good," he said. He stuck his tongue inside me.

"Oh god, that...that...that feels good," I said breathlessly. "That's erotic as hell. You're going to make me come fast," I said. He continued faster. "Angel. Oh god...please...oh!" I screamed his name as I came all over his tongue. He moved up to my mouth and smeared my juices all over my face.

"Oh, Angel," I whispered as I reached down and pulled his shirt over his head. "Angel, you're so damn hot." He reached down and pulled my dress over my head. He walked me over to his desk.

"Bend over, Bella. I want you like this," he said.

He unzipped his pants and pulled his cock out and aligned it to my slit. He pushed in fast, all the way to the balls, and grabbed me by the hips.

"You're so sexy bent over my desk and taking my big cock. It was made just for you."

"Oh god, you feel so good. Please, Angel," I said breathlessly. We both hit our orgasms at the same time.

"I love you, Bella, so much," he said breathlessly in my ear.

"I love you too."

"Let's go swimming with Giovanni and Grazia," he said.

We went out and swim with the family, and that seemed to have distracted Grazia from what happened earlier. We all enjoyed our day in the pool and at the playground. Amelia joined us as soon as his mother was escorted out. Things would be much better with her gone.

Angelino

We put together a huge party on neutral territory here in Chicago. All the wars would be left behind. We invited families from all over, allies and enemies. It was a place where they could discuss business and make alliances if necessary and reveal the seats of their tables. This party was to announce Annika's seat at the Rossi table and our cousins. Volkov would be there, and I wanted him to see how powerful Annika had become. But also, it would be the time we revealed who had been taking him down. Amelia would be at the party, so he would know.

Annika's sleeve was almost complete, leaving room for future children's names. There was a large phoenix rising from the ash and a reaper because she brought death. And there were flowers because she survived and was flourishing among several smaller ones. It was the sexiest thing I had ever seen. She radiated power more every day, and I loved her more every day. She had put on several pounds. She was still long and lean, but she worked out and had been building muscle. Her ass was a godsend. She had been training with my cousins and fighting and learning how to protect herself. They took it easy on her, saying she was pregnant. One thing about Annika, she was going be the best at everything.

"Good morning," Annika said as she walked in my office.

"Good morning yourself," I said, looking her over.

She was wearing a light yellow floral short-sleeve dress. It came right above her knees, and it was a V-neck. She had a pair of black wedge sandals on. She looked like she should be hanging out at the pool instead of my office today. She walked over to me, sat at my desk, bent over, and kissed me. I could see down her dress.

"You look beautiful," I said to her as she smiled at me.

"What are you up to today?" she asked.

"Just finishing invites for all the families. And you?"

"I was going to put the finishing touches in the office."

The office was huge. Being part of our castle, it was just a large room. She put in a huge square table seating sixteen people. She wanted everyone to feel equal, so this was there was no head of the table. There could also be a large leaf added if we continued to add more people. She put a lot of thought into the design. The table was black, and it matched the two double-sided disks. There were pictures of our Italian, Russian, and Greek heritage on the upper walls. And there were vintage weapons throughout. This was our war room.

"I think it turned out amazing."

"Thank you. I won't be bothering you then?" she said as she walked to the table.

"Not at all," I told her.

"Are you sure?" she asked as she looked over her shoulder at me, giving me that seductive smile.

Oh, she was up to something. She bent over at the waist, acting like she was picking something up off the floor. My mouth dropped open. She was not wearing any panties. I growled, rising from my chair.

"You little vixen. Me giving it to you twice last night wasn't enough?" She giggled.

"I don't know what you're talking about," she said innocently.

"Sure, you don't." I gave her a smile.

She turned around and put her hands on my chest. She reached up and kissed me. It turned passionate, and she reached down and unzipped my slacks and let them hit the floor. And then she shoved my underwear to the floor, and I stepped out of them. She left my button-down shirt on. She bit my lip, making my cock jump.

"God, Bella."

"Shhhhh," she cooed. "I've got you," she said, taunting me.

She unbuttoned my shirt and kissed her way down every button. She dropped to her knees. I looked down at her, and she was watching me. She grabbed my cock and started stroking it. I clenched my teeth.

"Damn, woman. The things you do to me."

She licked the tip of my cock, and I sucked in a breath. Then she put my dick in her mouth and shoved it down to the back of her throat, making me grab her hair.

"Fuck, Bella, please, you feel so fucking good."

I closed my eyes, savoring the feeling. I was huge, but she deep-throated me with ease, making sucking sounds. I started fucking her face.

"You're going make me cum if you don't stop."

She grabbed my ass and shoved it farther down her throat.

"Fuuuuckkk!" I bellowed as I came and put my seed down her throat. She swallowed most of it, and the rest of it and slobber were running down the sides of her mouth as she stared up at me.

"You are a god, woman."

She pulled my cock out of her mouth and stood, wiping her mouth with her fingers. She turned around and walked away until she got to the table. Looking at me, she jumped on the table and spread her legs wide.

"Eat my pussy, Angel. I need it."

Fuck if my cock didn't jump, ready again for round 2. I stalked over to her and kissed her hard, tasting my cum. She moaned.

"You want me to eat your pretty little pussy? Is my girl horny today?" I walked over to my desk and pulled out of a box. "I've got something for you," I said, opening the box. I pulled out a vibrator. She had the biggest grin.

"I've never used a toy."

"You're in for a treat."

I got on my knees and started licking her wet pussy. She was moaning and arching up for more. I stuck the vibrator inside her, and she moaned loudly.

"Oh…that…that feels so good. Oh, please, Angel, make me come," she begged.

I pulled the vibrator out of her pussy and put it on her clit.

"Oh shit. Oh fuck."

"You like that?" I stood up and pinched her nipple through her dress. I shoved my cock in one long stroke.

"Fuck my pussy, please. Hard," she whimpered.

"Hold the vibrator." She did, and I started slamming into her.

"I'm going to come, Angel. Don't stop." She screamed out my name.

As I continued to pound into her, I slowed my strokes, and she removed the vibrator. She threw her legs over my shoulders, and I continued in slow strokes.

"I want more," she whispered like she could never get enough.

I turned the vibrator back on and put it on her clit, and she started fucking me back.

"You like my cock in your pretty pussy? You like it hard and deep, don't you, Bella?" I started moving faster, and she started moaning louder. "Your pussy feels so good around my hard cock. Come for me, Bella. Milk my cock."

"Harder, please," she begged.

I grabbed her by the hips and slammed into her over and over until we both climaxed with a bellow. We lay there breathless for a minute, and then I pulled out and kissed her softly.

"Do you have any idea how much you mean to me?" I asked her. She looked at me.

"I pray as much as you mean to me," she said.

She laughed and looked at the table.

"Well, now that's all broken." It made me laugh out loud.

"Yes, it is. I love breaking in all the new furniture with you." I helped her off the desk and leaned down and kissed her belly that was starting to show. She now had a small baby bump.

We both put our clothes back on, and I put her in my lap and sat on my desk.

"Are you going to get a dress for the party?"

"Actually, Amelia is making both of our dresses. And she's also making Rachel's. She is an amazing designer. She made the dress I'm wearing."

"Really? She does have some talent."

"She really does. You're going to die when you see the dress she made for me. Giovanni wants to get her her own label, and we will be showcasing her dresses at the party."

Over the next month, we found out what Amelia owned in New York. Iris's father left it to her, and Amelia's father gave the other one-fourth to Leander. We decided to split the team in half and moved to New York. Giovanni, Leander, Dante, and Rocco moved to New York. They had been working on their house and flying back and forth, trying to get everything settled.

Annika

The brothers spoiled us women today. They brought the spa to us. Amelia, Rachel, and I all got ready at the house. We all had our nails done and French tips all the way around. We had our makeup professionally done, along with our hair.

Giovanni brought in a couple of high-end designer scouts to look at Amelia's designs tonight at the party. All three of us were wearing evening gowns tonight with three different designs. She also designed a rack of things back at the studio, if the designers decided they wanted to look.

Amelia's dress was designed in a mermaid butterfly Lisa Cammy style. It came above her knees, and it was in a light blue with rhinestones that sparkled and caught the light, matching her eyes. She had blue slingback stilettos to match. The dress went with her innocent and angel-like demeanor.

Rachel's dress was a V-neck double split thigh Cammy dress in black. It went well with her red hair perfectly. My dress was a red velvet, low plunge, and belted dress. The front split my breasts in a V, and it went way below my belly button. Then there was a belt in the same color velvet that matched. The front of the dress came halfway between my knee and my hips. The back of the dress cascaded down to the back of my heels. The dress was backless. It was absolutely stunning. It made me feel bold. I chose a black pair of open-toe slingbacks to go with it. My hair was half up and half down in long blond curls. On top of my head, I put a black crown with clear crystals. I wore red lipstick to match my dress with a smoky eye. My right arm was now finished from shoulder all the way to my fingertips and showcased the tattoos beautifully. I had never felt so confident.

Amelia had a wide silver halo on her head for the angel that she was with baby blue eye shadow that came to the outside of her eyes with shimmer. She looked like Cinderella.

We were the queens to our men. But also to the Mafia family. We had a photographer at the house, and one would be at the event. The men texted us and let us know that they had their tuxes on and were waiting in the living room. We headed down. We stopped on the balcony and then again on the staircase for the photographer. He told us to turn and pose, and then the men walked in.

Angelino

The girls spent the day getting ready for tonight's event. The men and I all spent the day going over security measures and making sure everything was set. Each person would go through a metal detector, and then they would be searched before entering. This event was for pleasure and business, not for violence. All families would announce new heads of the table, marriages and alliances, and whatever else was needed. This happened every few years.

The Rossis made big changes. We decided to initiate the party for this year. All the Rossis would be arriving together. We all had dates or beautiful wives. I couldn't wait to see everyone's faces when she was announced as head of the table. Hell, just when they would see her and her tattoos, her father would not recognize her. She was four months pregnant now and had not started showing much yet. She was now healthy and had a beautiful tall body with full breasts and ass.

Amelia was going with Giovanni. She was also four months pregnant. She was starting to show. Santos was bringing his fiery redhead, Rachel. We all knew he was in love with her. All the couples were here. We were waiting on Annika, Amelia, and Rachel to head down, and we would take the limo to the party. We would arrive about forty-five minutes late. I wanted to see everyone's faces when they saw Annika and Amelia.

We heard the photographer in the foyer talking, so the ladies must be coming down.

"Holly shit," someone said, and I heard men gasping. I came around them and looked up at the three women standing on the stairs.

"Jesus Christ," I said, looking at Annika.

"Damn, you guys are some lucky bastards," Luca said with his snotty girlfriend standing next to him. And all the other single guys said the same thing about our women. They all wished they had what we had.

The women were all stunning, but I had only eyes for Annika. I moved away from the guys and walked toward Annika, not being able to stop myself. She was a vision. I had never seen a more gorgeous, confident, powerful, fierce woman in my life.

I walked up the stairs and stood one step below her so we were close to the same height. I was kind of at a loss for words.

"Angel? Are you okay?"

I swallowed hard, looking in those beautiful blue eyes. "You're… you're sexy as hell. I can't comprehend what I'm looking at."

She was in a low-cut V-neck dress, the split all the way past her belly button, splitting her breast. The front of the dress was shorter than the back. It was a dress for a queen.

"You are my queen," I said, looking at her black crown.

"I'm not going to lie. I feel like a badass in this dress with my tattooed arm and crown," she said, laughing.

"You're more than a badass, Bella. So much more. My own cousins are jealous of me. And I'm sure I'm going to have to keep you close all night." She smiled. I kissed her red lips.

"I love you. You made this possible, Angel. I would not be who I am without you saving me."

"I'll save you for the rest of our lives. But who is going to save you from me? You in this dress is very dangerous. I just want to lick you starting at your belly button, between your breasts, and down again." She laughed.

"I guess the dress is a hit."

"You're royalty. You're so fucking fierce. You take my breath away."

"You're not hurting my eyes in this tux either. I just want to drop to my knees and suck your cock."

"Damn, Bella, you're making it hard to leave." We both laughed and started walking down the stairs. All the men told her how stunning she looked, and we headed to the car.

We were almost at the party, and I said, "Everyone, put your game faces on. We are going to piss Volkov off as soon as we walk in. He will see Rachel and Amelia. And then I'm sure I'll piss them off later." She winked at me, and everybody laughed.

A couple of our cousins stepped out of the car first so they could spot Volkov. We had a plan and wanted Annika to distract him while the other two women got inside.

"He is to your left at the bar with his new top man, James," Luca said as he stepped aside and let me lead Annika in. She had her arm on mine.

He looked at us when we walked in and passed over Annika. He looked at me and then looked back at Annika, not realizing that the woman on my arm was his daughter. He gazed up and down her body, assessing this new Annika. Annika did the same to him and then turned her eyes to me like he was not important enough to give her time to.

"How about a drink, sexy?" I smiled at her and walked her to the bar. I ordered a whiskey because she was a badass. We both had her drinks, and her father and James made their way over. They stopped about four feet from us.

"You have outdone yourself with the party, Rossi," Volkov said, making small talk. Amelia and Rachel were in the corner behind him with Giovanni and Santos waiting for my nod.

"It's about time all the families got together," I said to him. I brought the glass to her lips and took a big sip while her father watched her.

"Annika, you're not going to give your papa hug?"

She laughed out loud and smiled at him. "I don't think I will, Daddy dearest," she said with a sarcastic voice, making me laugh.

"You look radiant," James told her, and her father turned to him, pissed for talking about his daughter. Annika pushed her father's buttons.

"You've always been so sweet, James. Thank you." I was dying inside. She was causing an inside feud. Her father's teeth were gritted.

"What is your plan for the buildings on Lake Michigan?" Volkov asked, changing the subject.

Annika answered, knowing it would piss him off. "They will be high-end penthouses for some of our men. The large empty building will be my clinic."

He glared at her, daring her to speak. "I see. So you're a doctor or something, right?"

She laughed at him. "Yes. Dr. Rossi." He did not like the name change. "So, Daddy, why don't you just say what's on your mind? It's written all over your face."

Looking at me, he said, "Our women are not allowed to speak. You need to keep a chain on her mouth." Annika and I both laughed.

"Oh, where is the fun in that? Come on, Dad. You don't like me having a voice?" Then she got fierce and glared at him. "Let me tell you this, old man. I have a lot more than just a voice. More than just a gorgeous face and ass. Let me tell you who I am. I am Angelino Rossi's wife. I am Grazia's mother. I'm the mother of the child I'm carrying and any other future heirs that will rule behind us. I'm Dr. Annika Rossi. I am a Russian princess. But most of all, I'm Annika fucking Rossi, Mafia queen. And when I come to end you, you'll beg for your life."

He glared at her.

"I have a surprise for you, Daddy."

I nodded, and both women and Giovanni and Santos walked over with Amelia's father.

"Do you remember Apollo Argyros?" Annika asked.

He saw him and started to greet him when his daughter stepped up beside him with Giovanni.

"Choose your words wisely, Pops. I see those wheels turning. You don't want to upset anyone now, do you?" Annika said with sarcasm, knowing her father wanted to say something smart. "Let me introduce Amelia Rossi, Giovanni's wife," Annika said.

Annika started laughing after seeing the look on her father's face. He didn't know what to say. Then Santos and Rachel walked up. Rachel was a hellcat and could speak for herself.

"Mr. Volkov, we meet again," Rachel said.

"So we do. What's the meaning of this?" Things started clicking in his head.

"Don't worry, Rachel. Everyone knows you would have beat his old ass if he hadn't had his man holding you. But I'll give you that chance before I end his life," Annika said, and Rachel smiled. "So, Pops, it's all starting to click together now? Because you're sure not as cocky as I remember. Okay, if you're that stupid, then I can spell it out for you. Volkov Mafia is no more." She looked over at James. "He is broke. I have all his money and all his properties that were in my name. Thanks, by the way, Daddy. That was very smart of you." She taunted him with her words.

"What the fuck are you talking about?" he asked.

"I took all your money and burned your properties to the ground." Annika said, laughing a sadistic laugh. "Just think of the money as payment for trying to break me. But the joke's on you. It looks like your little alliance has created a bit of a monster. So listen up, you fat fuck. I'm claiming my seat as one of the heads of the Rossi table tonight. Then I'm coming for you. We are going to take you apart piece by piece for all the attacks on my daughter's life and the hell you put these women through. James, I would get the hell away from my father and get the hell out of town if I were you," Annika said to them both.

We had killed most of their men, so they held their tongues. They didn't have any backup here. They turned away and walked off. All the women burst out laughing. I leaned into Annika's ear.

"My cock is as hard as a rock right now. I love your dirty mouth. I need it on my cock."

She swung around and pressed her body to mine. She reached down and grabbed both of my ass cheeks as she kissed me with passion.

"God, you drive me crazy. You made me like this," she said, making me laugh.

"I fucking love it."

The night continued. We danced and drank. All the families announced their table heads, and then it was the Rossis' turn. I walked up on stage, and all my cousins walked out and gave each of the names and let the families know that they all held equal power. Giovanni brought Amelia onstage.

"This is Amelia Rossi, formally Amelia Argyros, my beautiful wife. She is better known to our people as the angel of Chicago. She holds a seat next to me as protector of our people." And they cheered.

Annika was still on the floor with everyone. I crooked my finger and motioned for her to come to me. She walked up on the stage and stepped to me. I kissed her softly and then turned her to everyone.

"I have one last announcement. This is my gorgeous wife, Annika Rossi. She is my queen and will have a head seat at the table beside me." There were gasps through the air. She stood tall and fierce.

Giovanni bent down on one knee and bowed to her. Then all the women and all my men followed. Holy shit, I was not expecting that. I heard about it happening with Amelia a couple of months back. Annika grabbed my hand and lifted our hands in the air.

"We are the Rossis. We are many, but we rule as one," she said, and all our people stood up and started cheering and running up to Annika. I looked over at her father, and he looked like he might be sick.

We headed home and went to our room.

"They bowed to me. I was not expecting that."

"They love you. You saved our daughter and continue to amaze everyone. They all respect you to no end."

"It's kind of hot," she said, laughing.

"You're not getting a big head, are you?" I asked her. Then we both laughed.

"There is only one big head I want," she said, palming my cock through my tux.

Volkov

I had been looking forward to this party. I wanted to see my daughter. I couldn't wait to end the Argyroses then the Rossis and get her back. I might have to bring her back sooner. All the other women didn't compare to her. I couldn't wait to touch her tonight. She would always be mine. My little princess who always did what she was told.

I waited with James at the party for the Rossis to show up. I needed Annika. I could make her leave with me for a bit if I could just touch her. She would be scared and do what I want.

James elbowed me in the side, and I looked up at the couple entering. A sexy blond and, wait, that's Angelino. I looked back at the blond. That was Annika. She looked nothing like my Annika. This one was built, and she had a tattoo from her shoulder to her fingertips. She looked like she owned this place. What the hell did he do to her? They walked over to the bar and ordered drinks. James and I made our way over. I needed to get her alone. I needed to touch her.

We made small talk, and I watched Annika drink whiskey. Whiskey? She did not drink. I could see skin from her neck down to her navel. Where was the rest of her dress?

I tried talking to her, but she only mocked me and taunted me. Where did she learn such language? She acted like a Mafia don.

James had been slobbering over my daughter. She thanked him for always being kind. How kind had he been? He would pay for ever touching my daughter.

She laughed at me and didn't even call me Papa anymore. I was pissed. I walked to the corner and watched all the heads make their announcements. I was fuming over the way Annika spoke to me.

That bitch thinks she can speak to me that way. I will get her back and rip that child from her stomach.

I watched as they danced and kissed and laughed. He loved her. She was a weakness. Or she would be if she was not going to be head of the table. My daughter? A head of a rival Mafia? I should have made her one of ours instead of losing her. He needed to get his hands off her.

The Rossis went onstage. How many heads did they have? This was not good. I would have to cut off nine heads to bring them down. He took my daughter onstage and announced her seat, and the entire crowd gasped.

Yeah, you're weak. They all know it with a woman as a head. Wait, are they all bowing to her? What the hell.

"Sir, this is not good. I've seen that type of loyalty and power. They admire her. They're going to serve her," James said, shocked.

Angelino

Over the next two months, we worked on taking Volkov down. He disappeared after the party when he realized he no longer had an alliance and everybody was against him. Our cousins moved out after they got the penthouses secured. Every time we got close to Volkov, he was gone before we got there. Leander and Giovanni were here helping with a few issues before he headed back to New York.

"Hey, Angelino, what's wrong?" Annika asked as she entered the office.

"I'm frustrated. I can't find your father. Being locked down so long is wearing me down. I worry about you being stuck here."

"I'm fine, Angel. I have everything I need. Let's be honest, I'm getting fat. Nobody wants to see that," she said, laughing.

"You're barely showing at six months, and you're sexy as hell pregnant. I may have to keep you this way." She sat down in my lap. "We have used all our resources trying to find him. We even checked properties in your name, and we came across nothing. He didn't leave, or we would know it. He no longer has a jet or money, so he couldn't have gone very far. I don't know. I'm just so exhausted."

"We will find him. I promise you that, Angel."

"I do have a doctor's appointment today. A routine checkup. I'll take the four bodyguards with me and then come straight back. When are you meeting with the city on the building permits?" she asked.

"In about thirty minutes. I'm sorry I can't make this appointment. I'll be home as soon as I can. Kiss me, wife. I have to go."

She kissed me. She headed to her doctor's appointment, and I headed to my meeting.

Annika

I went in for my six-month checkup. I had a small baby bump. You could see it when I wore a pencil skirt like the one I had on today. I walked into my appointment, and they took me straight back as usual. The guards secured the outside doors and the door to the back where Leander was. No one was allowed back when I was there. I sat on a table. A nurse came in to take my vitals. Then the doctor came in before I got undressed to explain what was going to happen during my exam today.

"We're going to take some blood today, and we'll do that first before your exam. I'll send the nurse, and then you can change your clothes."

A little blond nurse came back in.

"What arm works better for you?" she asked me in a nervous voice.

"Either one is fine."

She laid out vials and needles. She stuck the needle in my arm.

"This is flush," she said. And as soon as it went in my arm, I knew something was wrong.

"What was..." I said. The nurse had tears in her eyes.

"I'm sorry, but he has my daughter," she said as whatever she gave me took over. She helped me lay back and walked out. A couple of goons walked in, and I blacked out.

Angelino

"What's wrong?" I said, answering my phone.

"They took her from the clinic," Leander said into the phone.

"How the fuck did they take her? Where is she? Did you call Luca?" I said in a panic.

"They slipped her through a side window after drugging her. When it took longer than it should have, we went to the back, and the doctor was tied in an exam room. He said they had him at gunpoint. They brought some nurse in to drug her, and two goons took her. I'm working on finding the nurse now."

"You better find her. And keep me posted. Fuck!" I screamed. I couldn't think.

"I'll handle it, Angelino. We will get her back. I'll get the team on it," Giovanni said, sitting next to me.

"Look, we need surveillance around Annika's clinic. I need everything you have. There was a nurse they used to gain entry, with blond hair. She was working with him. Get a team on this," Giovanni said to him.

"We got it." He hung up. Thirty minutes later, Luca called Giovanni as I paced the floor.

"We know who she is. Emma Carter. She was kidnapped when she was nineteen. Her aunt reported her missing. She was taken from a trailer park in Arkansas. Face recognition saw her going into an apartment building on the east side. Graceland Apartments. We have Leander sitting on the apartments with three other men. She got off on the second floor. There are six apartments on the floor. Only two have tenants," he said.

"Send them in. Bring her back here," Giovanni said.

They headed up to the second floor and spread out. They listened at all the doors. Noise came from only one. Orion picked the lock, and Leander headed in first. The apartment was tiny with one bedroom about five hundred square feet. It was old and in horrible shape. She was pacing back and forth in front of the window. The wig she was wearing was on the chair. She turned around and screamed as soon as she saw Leander pointing the gun at her. She cried. She was a small little thing with dirty black hair and green eyes. She was about five five.

"On your knees," Leander said.

She dropped to her knees and was shaking badly.

"Where did they take her?" Leander asked.

"I don't know. They didn't tell me. They…they just told me what to do," she said.

"Yeah, and you did it," Leander said to her with disgust in his voice. He thought she was beautiful. What kind of person did that to a pregnant woman?

"I didn't have a choice," she said.

"There is always a choice," he told her. "You're going to walk out of here with me like we are best friends. Anything crazy and I'll leave you dead. Do you understand me?"

"Yes," she whispered. We left her apartment and headed down.

"Emma," a woman said.

She turned to look at the woman. "Yes."

"Where is Lily?"

"With friends," she said. "We have to go."

"Good job, princess," Leander said to her.

She must know she's going to die. She's not even fighting, like she just has given up, Leander thought to himself.

Annika

I woke up with a huge headache. I was lying on my side. When I was able to focus, I realized I was in a cell of sorts, and I was lying on concrete.

"Well, she's finally awake." It was a voice I recognized as my father. I looked out the door.

"Welcome home, daughter," he said with sarcasm. I said nothing. "Are you not happy to see your father?"

"Where am I?" I asked him.

"It used to be an old clinic I owned under your mother's name. I retrofitted these cells for my special guests."

No GPS signal would get through these walls. He stepped in the cell. I stayed on the floor and pulled my knees to my chest to protect my son.

"Afraid of dear old dad?" he said. He slumped down and punched me hard. I stayed in my position. "We are going to get reacquainted soon, and then that child you're carrying will be sold off at an auction to the biggest child molester I can find." He laughed.

I stayed calm and thought, *He is nothing but a big bully that likes to pick on women. Come up with a plan.*

"But first, before we have this fun, we're going to make a few videos."

He walked out of the cell and locked the door. He walked away, and I got up and walked around, seeing if I could find something. There was another cell next to mine with a man sitting on the floor, his hands chained to the wall. His head was down. He had long black hair and tattoos everywhere. He was muscular but looked like they were starving him.

"Hey, can you hear me?"

He didn't move. He had blood on his chest. They must have been beat him up recently, maybe knocked him out.

Angelino

"They took the girl to the dungeon," Giovanni said.

We headed down to the dungeon. They put the girl in the cell.

God, she is young, I thought to myself.

"How old are you?" I asked.

"Twenty-one," she said in a low voice with fear in her eyes.

"If you answer my questions, this will be a lot more pleasant. You'll pay either way for kidnapping my wife," I told her.

She backed up against the wall. "Are you going to kill me?" she asked in a tiny voice.

"Most likely," I said. Leander was pacing like a caged animal.

"Where did they take my wife?"

"I don't know. He never talked in front of me," she said.

"What happened?" I asked her, and she said nothing. "Answer me!" I yelled, and she started shaking. She looked at the floor. She looked like my wife when I brought her here. I opened the cell.

"You fucking bitch, you better tell me something or it ends here," I told her.

She sobbed. "I can't."

I grabbed her by her arms and shook her. She peed herself. Leander put an arm on mine.

"Wait, boss." He pointed at her chest. "She is leaking milk." I released her.

"Open your eyes." And she did. "Are you pregnant?"

She shook her head no.

"Do you have a child?" I asked.

She looked so lost, and tears spilled over. She had her head down, staring at her feet. I knew Leander was chomping at the bit to help her. I nodded at him. He picked her up in his arms. He looked broken to see her left that way. Just like I did.

"Let me know what you need for her. We'll send food up in a little bit."

"Thank you," he said and headed to his room.

I rubbed my hand over my face.

Annika

I heard a door open and then a screaming baby. My father walked in and opened my cell door.

"Take her. She won't shut the fuck up. You can take care of her. Make her stop crying," he said.

"Who is she?"

"Your sister."

"Oh my god, I need supplies, her bottle, and diapers," I told him.

"My guys will bring it. At least your stupid ass will be useful for something."

His words didn't hurt me anymore. He left, and I walked around with the baby to try to calm her down. My sister. Wow. I wondered where her mother was. She had black hair and blue eyes. She was beautiful.

"What's your name, pretty girl?" I asked her.

The guard came in with a carrier and water and formula and diapers.

"I need a milk warmer."

The guard brought a teapot in and plugged it in in the corner outside the cell.

"Do you know what her name is?" I asked.

"Lily," he said and walked out.

I poured some water in the pot and turned it on. I changed her diaper. She had a nasty diaper rash. I looked through the bag and found some cream. I cleaned her up, put on some cream, and put her in a new diaper. I rocked her against me, and she finally quieted down.

"That's it, Lily. Did your bottom hurt?" I said.

I made her a bottle, and she drank it and fell asleep in my arms.

"You're so beautiful. I pray your mommy is safe." I lay her down in her carrier, and she slept and didn't move.

The guy in the cell next to me started to move around, and he lifted his head and blinked several times.

He looks familiar, I thought to myself. He had shoulder-length hair and blue eyes.

"You're the daughter," he said. "Welcome to the party."

I laughed. "Well, by the looks of you, the party has gotten rowdy."

He chuckled and winced in pain, probably from broken ribs.

"My name is Annika. What's yours?" I asked.

"Antonio Rossi," he said.

I looked at him like he was nuts. "Is this a joke?" I asked.

"What are you talking about?" he asked.

"You're Antonio Rossi from the Rossi Mafia? You died a year ago," I asked.

"That's me, but I was not killed. I was kidnapped and interrogated," he said.

"Oh my god, your brothers think you're dead. They're going to be so happy. All they talk about is you," I said.

"What do you know of my brothers? You're Russian."

I laughed. I was careful about what I said just in case the room was bugged. "I'm Annika Rossi, Angelino's wife," I said.

He looked at me. "Really? How are they?"

"They miss you every day. Your brothers and cousins took over in your absence, and now they run it united."

"He was always meant to bring the family around. I never wanted it. I hated it. I wonder what your father's plan is," he asked.

"I'm certain it's sadistic, whatever it is."

"Is that your baby?" he asked.

"No. He said she was my sister and handed her to me. But I am pregnant."

"Congratulations. My brother's going have another kid."

"Yes, a son. And Giovanni adopted a little girl, and his wife is pregnant."

"I have missed out on so much. I just pray I get out of here so I can have kids one day," he said.

"Oh, we're getting the hell out of here."

"I don't know how. He's here every day," he said.

"That just means we're not far. He took me yesterday, so we are very close."

Leander

"Shhh, it's okay. I'm taking you to my room. I'll get you cleaned up, and then we can talk," I said.

I just pulled her to my chest. I knew she had been through something horrible. I could see it now. And she had a child she was not with. I opened the door and closed it behind me. I walked into the bathroom and set her on her feet. I ran her a bath.

"Get undressed and get in. I'll get you some clothes. What do I need to get you for your breast leaking?"

"I need a breast pump," she said with her head down and crying.

"You're safe. I know it doesn't feel like it, but you are. I'll get you what you need, and then we'll eat and talk. Get in, princess. Get in and relax."

I left and closed the door. I got a pair of my sweats and a shirt for her. I knocked on the door and cracked it open.

"I'm going to slide your clothes in on the floor."

I put them on the floor. Vera and a few guards went to town and got her some women's stuff. She was still in the bathroom when I got back. I knocked on the door.

"Are you okay?" I asked.

"Yes," she said.

"Here is the pump and some other things you may need. I'll be back out here. Dinner is on its way up."

"Thank you," she said.

"You're welcome, princess." I closed the door.

Fifteen minutes later, she emerged from the bathroom smelling like my body wash. She stood by the door.

"It's okay. You can sit anywhere."

There was a fireplace and sofa and chairs like the rest of the rooms. She sat in a chair and tucked her feet underneath her. I lit the fireplace because she was trembling. I grabbed a blanket off the couch and covered her up. Vera knocked and walked in with our food and set it on the coffee table.

"Thank you, Vera." She walked out. "Let's see what the chef made. Looks like a steak and potato tonight."

She was extremely underweight. She sat down on the floor in front of the coffee table, and I did the same. We ate the silence. When she finished, I started talking.

"I know you were kidnapped two years ago. Tell me what happened," I said. She said nothing. "I believe you don't know anything about Annika. I believe you were forced to assist," I said.

"Yes, I was." She was talking.

"How old is your child?"

"She is three months," she said with tears in her eyes.

I put my hand on hers. "What's her name?"

"Lily," she said.

"Where is she?" She didn't answer that. "I won't let anyone hurt you. Just let me help you."

"He took her," she said. "Pavel Volkov has my daughter. He had me in his house. He knew I was taking nursing classes when he kidnapped me. He kept my daughter and put me in that apartment. He told me I would not get her back if I didn't do what he said. He will do the same things he has done to me to her. I must get her back, please," she said.

"We'll get her back. Who's the father?" I asked.

"Pavel. He raped me," she said and put her head down.

I picked her up off the floor and sat her in my lap in the chair.

"We will get her back. I promise, princess. You're safe with me."

Annika

My father walked in.

"Well, I guess we're all caught up on the family reunion." He put his phone through the cell and snapped a picture of me. "Well, let me send this to your hubby just to piss him off."

My eye was swollen shut from the punch. My father walked in the cell.

"Well, now on to the next part of my evil plan." He looked over at Antonio. "You're going to die today by Annika's hand, and I'll send your body to their doorstep," he said, and my heart stopped. I must stop this.

"Come, daughter. Come on. We're going to have some fun with your brother-in-law before you kill him. Angelino will hate you for killing his brother."

My sister was in her carrier in the corner of the cell. I took a deep breath because I knew I could take him, pregnant or not. He walked up to me and grabbed me by both arms. Before I could think better of it, I leaned back and headbutted him as hard as I could, shattering his nose. Then I came up with a knee and kicked him in the nuts. He dropped to the floor with a grunt. I grabbed the baby and her bag and set them outside the cell. I grabbed a hammer off the table against the wall.

I looked down at my father as he was covered in blood. I hit him on the side of the jaw with a hammer, not enough to knock him out. He looked at me in disbelief.

"Well, Pops, it looks like you got yourself in a bit of a predicament," I said, taunting him. "You were always a weak fucker. What did I tell you when I found you? What would happen to you? You don't die today, Pops. We're going to torture you for months for what you've done. Your reign is over, and mine has just begun."

And I swung out and hit him hard across the jaw with a hammer, knocking him out. I took everything out of the cell that he could use to try to get out and removed his keys, gun, and his cell phone. I took them with me when I locked the cell behind me.

I opened Antonio's cell and removed his restraints.

"That was extremely impressive. I guess I don't need to worry about where your loyalties lie," he said, making us both laugh.

"Never," I said. "Can you stand? We need to get out of here." I helped him stand.

He walked around and moved his arms around. He was stiff. He took the gun. I picked up my sister and slung the diaper bag over my shoulder. He headed out in front of me. He stepped out the door. There was no one here. We were in a metal building, like a shipping container, with a door added to it. There was an SUV left there. I walked over, and the key was in it. I put the baby in his arms, and I got in the driver's seat. I backed out and headed down the street.

"Wait, I know where I am. The mansion is ten minutes from here." I pulled out, made sure no one was following me, and drove toward the mansion.

Angelino

Luca came running in the office where I had been since Annika was taken two days ago.

"Her GPS just popped back up. She is five minutes from here. They're heading this way," he said.

"What the hell? Oh god," I said.

"She's alive. She's going to be fine," Giovanni said to me, trying to keep me focused.

He was thinking the same thing I was. That they were throwing a body at our gate. We all headed outside and left the women in the house. A vehicle pulled up to the gate. I ran, and it was Annika driving. Thank God she was alive. She put it in park and ran to me and jumped in my arms. Guards had the guns aimed on the passenger. She was covered in blood.

"Are you okay? How did you get away?"

"I'm fine. This is not my blood." I held her tight, afraid she was not real.

"Who is with you?" I asked her, and she looked behind her and realized that she had a passenger still in the vehicle with guns on him.

"Oh god," she said. "Drop your guns now." They did as she said.

She turned to me and Giovanni and smiled. She grabbed my hands.

"I don't know how to tell you guys this. That's Antonio," she said. We both looked at her. "It's your brother. He's not dead."

We both looked at the car at the same time. And we both moved fast toward the car.

Antonio got out of the SUV. Antonio had tears falling down his face and walked up and embraced Giovanni and me. I don't think there was a dry eye around. I was crying. Giovanni was crying.

I watched Annika, and she grabbed a baby out of the car. Leander walked up to her.

"Her name is not Lily, by any chance?" he asked.

"Yes. How did you know?" Annika replied.

"Her mother is in my room. May I take her to her mother?" Leander took the baby and headed back to the house.

My brothers and I still embraced. Annika started giving out orders.

"Rocco, my father is in a warehouse ten minutes from here. It looks like a couple shipping containers. Follow the GPS and bring them back here and secure them in the basement. The place used to be an old medical clinic."

"I'm on it," Rocco said, taking a couple of guys with him.

"Take the baby stuff to Leander, please."

"Yes, ma'am," the guard said. The cousins headed back in the house. The brothers separated.

"How are you alive? What happened to you? How did you end up with my wife?"

Annika laughed and said, "Let's go in the house. Get him food and drinks, and we can talk."

I grabbed Annika. "I'm so glad you're safe. And you brought my brother back from the dead."

"She actually saved my life, her sister's life and hers, and her baby," Antonio said.

I stopped in my tracks. "How did you manage to save all of them?" I asked her.

"'Your reign is over, and mine has just begun,'" Antonio said. "That is what your wife told him when she smacked him across the face with a hammer and knocked him out." This made me laugh.

"My queen, your reign will last a lifetime." I kissed her.

I could finally breathe again with Annika back, and she saved her sister and my brother. She took out Volkov single-handedly. Rocco picked him up and secured him in the basement.

We all headed in the house, and the chef fed Antonio. We spent several hours going over how he survived the torture Volkov put him through. We told him about New York and all the changes we had made. He told me how fierce my wife was. He met sweet Amelia, and our family was now complete. We let him shower, and Annika looked him over, and we let him rest. I was afraid to sleep because this might be a dream, and Antonio might not be here when I woke up.

"Bella, I need to build you a throne. That way, you can reign over our people. You think they loved you before. Now you saved my brother and yourself. You are now untouchable."

"I pray I'm not untouchable because I have not had sex in days, and I'm dying," she said, making me laugh.

"Damn, woman, can you ever get enough?"

"Not of your sexy ass, I can't."

That night, we made love, sweet and gentle, and I savored every inch of her beautiful body. This woman was everything to me and my family. We made love a couple of times through the night because neither of us could sleep.

Leander

I headed down to the gate when the team told us Annika's GPS came back up. A car came flying up to the gate, and Annika stepped out, running to Angelino. The guards kept their guns on the passenger of the car. Anna gave orders for them to back down. That it was their brother they thought was dead. Annika pulled the baby out of the back seat of the car. I walked over to Annika.

"Is that Lily, by any chance?" I asked.

"Yes. How do you know that?"

"Her mother is in my room. May I take her to see her mother?"

Annika handed the baby to me, and I cradled Lily to my chest. I locked Emma in my room. She had been through a lot, and I didn't want her trying to run. I unlocked the door and stepped in. She was in the bathroom.

"Emma, can you come out for a minute?" I asked her.

"Yes. Give me a minute," she replied.

"Don't pump your breasts yet," I told her.

"What?" And she stepped out of the bathroom and saw the baby.

"Oh my god, is that…" She ran up to me and looked to see if it was Lily. "It's Lily. How did you find her?"

I handed Lily over to her. She looked at me with suspicion like I had her the entire time.

"Annika, the woman we were looking for, she knocked Volkov out and escaped. She had the baby with her." Emma was crying so hard.

"Thank you. Thank you," she said, gratefully reuniting with her baby.

Angelino

We headed down early and had the chefs make a huge breakfast for everyone. We met in the huge dining room. Antonio walked in smiling with his hair in a man bun. It wasn't a dream. He was alive. Annika put in orders to the chef to make sure Antonio got plenty of protein to help put muscle back on him.

"God, it's good to be home," Antonio said.

Grazia ran in and jumped in his lap. She remembered him.

"Where is Mother?" Antonio asked.

"In the dungeon, awaiting her execution," I told him. I explained her involvement in everything. He nodded in understanding.

"After breakfast, I would like to pay them both a visit," Antonio said, not wasting any time on ending this.

"There is going to be a huge line of people who want a piece of them both," Giovanni said.

Amelia walked around the table and whispered something in Antonio's ear. He looked up at her and then to Giovanni and smiled. Amelia walked around the table and put a piece of paper in front of us. It was a family crest.

"What's this?" I asked.

"If the table approves it, it will be our family crest. We can each have it tattooed. Our men will all have it so it can be seen," Amelia said.

"This is a great idea. If anyone betrays us, we remove it," Annika said, making me laugh at how ruthless she was.

We all enjoyed each other's company and headed down to the dungeon.

"Are you two ready for a bit of fun?" Dante asked our guests.

Our mother looked up and saw Antonio.

"How did you escape?" Then she shut her mouth fast, realizing she just screwed up.

"I may not need Orion for this job," I said.

"You had your son kidnapped and tortured. What the hell is wrong with you?" Giovanni screamed at her.

"This family belongs to me. I should be running it."

"You won't be alive long enough to see how well this family runs without you and our father. We never loved you either, Mother, and there will not be a tear lost over your torture and death," I told her.

Volkov was chained to the wall naked.

"Remember everything you did to these women and my brother?" I asked him. He glared at me. "It will be handed down to you tenfold over the next few weeks. You're the weakest man I have ever seen. Taken down by your own daughter. How pathetic."

He and our mother were in the basement for weeks. Everything Volkov did to these women was done to him. We left our mother in Orion's hands, and she suffered. On week 4, we ended both of their pathetic lives. They would never darken our lives again. Amelia and Annika were both six months pregnant. And all was calm for now. Antonio was trying to adjust to being home. He traveled back and forth from here to New York.

"I love you so much, Bella. Our life is perfect."

"I love you, Angel. I got my fairytale ending."

About the Author

Cynthia Seidel took her love for reading to a new level and decided to write her own novels. Writing has been an escape from anxiety and depression for this new but talented writer. She raised two daughters on her own and worked men's jobs to survive and take care of her girls. Life was a struggle and challenge. It's a life she fought tooth and nail to overcome. She was raised in the backwoods of Saratoga, Arkansas, and then later moved to Hope, Arkansas. She now resides on a small ranch in South Texas, where she fell in love with her husband of ten years and wanted other women to experience that fierce love and loyalty through her books. With the support of her husband and two daughters, her dream is now a reality. She wanted every woman to know it's never too late to make a dream come true, keep fighting, and never give up. She wanted to be an example for all women of all ages.

Printed in the USA
CPSIA information can be obtained
at www.ICGtesting.com
LVHW091124100724
785083LV00004B/187